Lying for love . . .

"Hi," Jessica said shyly, stooping down to Dennis's level. "You're Dennis, right?"

Dennis looked up. "Do I know you?"

Jessica shrugged. "Not really," she told him. Which was the understatement of the century. "But I know you. I'm—um—" She swallowed hard. "Elizabeth. Wakefield, that is." There. She'd done it.

Dennis nodded solemnly. "Nice to meet you."

"Nice to meet you," Jessica said. "Listen, I, um, wanted to talk to you about something."

Dennis gazed out across the lake and splashed the water with his bare heel. "Sure," he said. "What is it?"

Jessica steeled her nerves. "It's about my, um, sister."

Dennis raised his eyebrows and swiveled to face Jessica. "You have a sister? Is she here at camp?"

Jessica nodded. That much was true anyway. "Her name's Jessica," she said brightly. "She looks just like me, only she's, you know, cleaner? And, um, a tiny bit prettier. I mean, we're identical twins, but we don't look exactly alike," she lied. "Everybody always says Jessica is prettier than I am." And if they don't, they should.

Dennis nodded slowly. "Uh-huh," he said. "So, um, how am I going to get to know this sister of yours?"

He's buying it! Jessica thought excitedly.

Visit the Official Sweet Valley Web Site on the Internet at:

http://www.sweetvalley.com

SWEET VALLEY TWINS
◇ SUPER EDITION ◇

Jessica's First Kiss

Written by
Jamie Suzanne

Created by
FRANCINE PASCAL

BANTAM BOOKS
NEW YORK · TORONTO · LONDON · SYDNEY · AUCKLAND

RL 4, 008-012

JESSICA'S FIRST KISS
A Bantam Book / April 1997

*Sweet Valley High® and Sweet Valley Twins® are
registered trademarks of Francine Pascal.*

Conceived by Francine Pascal.

*Produced by Daniel Weiss Associates, Inc.
33 West 17th Street
New York, NY 10011.*

Cover art by Bruce Emmett.

ISBN: 0-553-48392-7

Published simultaneously in the United States and Canada

Bantam Books are published by Bantam Books, a division of Bantam
Doubleday Dell Publishing Group, Inc. Its trademark, consisting of the
words "Bantam Books" and the portrayal of a rooster, is Registered in the
U.S. Patent and Trademark Office and in other countries. Marca
Registrada. Bantam Books, 1540 Broadway, New York, New York 10036.

PRINTED IN THE UNITED STATES OF AMERICA

OPM   0 9 8 7 6 5 4 3 2 1

To Jenevieve Terese Campo

One

◇

"I'm really psyched about going to camp tomorrow," Jessica Wakefield said to her best friend, Lila Fowler. "How about you?"

It was Saturday morning, and the girls were lounging on the couch in Jessica's living room. The next afternoon Jessica, Lila, and all the other kids in Sweet Valley Middle School would be boarding buses to spend a week at a campground called Bannerman's Estate.

The trip would be fun, Jessica thought. If nothing else, it would be a chance to get away from her obnoxious older brother, Steven. And it would be cool hanging with her friends. And although camp would be outdoors, with no VCRs or microwave ovens, she could get into canoe rides, swimming, moonlight, and all that other good stuff. "So what do you think, Lila?" she asked.

Lila laughed. "Camp is going to be *so* cool," she said, giving Jessica a conspiratorial wink. "We're going to have a truly awesome time."

Jessica was a little surprised to hear Lila sound so positive. Lila was the richest girl in Sweet Valley, and she liked all the comforts of home—especially *her* home, Fowler Mansion. "So what do you think should be so awesome about it, exactly?" Jessica asked skeptically.

"Well." Lila plucked a stray thread off one of the couch pillows. "First of all, no school for a whole week."

"That's true," Jessica agreed. "We will have to take classes once in a while, though," she said glumly. "All about nature and the history of Bannerman's Estate and other deadly stuff like that."

Lila nodded. "Can't you just see Mrs. Arnette lecturing the whole school?"

Jessica laughed. "Now, students," Jessica said, imitating their social studies teacher, "until the railroad ran through here, the pioneers relied upon sauerkraut for all their nutritional needs." She stuck her finger in the air, lifted her chin, and fluttered her eyelashes furiously. "They ate sauerkraut for breakfast, lunch, and dinner. They even used money made out of sauerkraut."

"Oh, they did not either," Lila said impatiently.

Jessica snickered. She liked the idea of money being made out of sauerkraut. "No, you're probably right. History's never that good."

Lila shrugged. "But no one's giving us grades," she pointed out. "And anyway, that's just a little bit of the day. The rest of the time we'll kick back and relax."

Kick back and relax. The idea sounded great to Jessica. "Yeah," she said happily. "Maybe they'll have floating rafts and stuff on the lake. We can lie out there and soak up rays and—"

"Rafts on the lake?" Lila stared at Jessica curiously. "Who needs rafts on the lake? I meant the tanning salon. A Jacuzzi. Things like that."

It was Jessica's turn to stare. "A Jacuzzi?" she asked. "Are there Jacuzzi baths at Bannerman's Estate?"

Lila snorted contemptuously. "Of course there are, doofus! Don't you know what an estate is? Haven't you ever been to one before?"

"Huh?" Jessica blinked. "Well, sure. An estate is, like, a big place. It's got lots of ground and trees and maybe a river." Her hands sketched hills and valleys in the air. "We went camping once at an old estate near the ocean. Me and Elizabeth and Steven and my parents. A couple of years ago." Elizabeth, her twin sister, had had the best time of anybody, she remembered. But that was Elizabeth. She was the kind of kid who could be happy even when it rained.

While Jessica and Elizabeth looked exactly alike, each with long blond hair, blue-green eyes, and a dimple in her cheek, they weren't alike at all on the inside. Jessica loved being the center of attention, and she lived for her friends. She was a member of the most exclusive club at Sweet Valley Middle

School, the Unicorn Club. In fact, come to think of it, she'd been a little bored on that camping trip because there just weren't enough kids around. Elizabeth, on the other hand, preferred to spend her time with one or two close friends, and she didn't usually mind being alone. Jessica loved shopping malls, fashion, and parties, while Elizabeth was most comfortable writing stories or curled up with a good book. Despite their differences, though, the girls were the best of friends.

Lila sighed. "Don't you know *anything?*" she asked. "An estate has lots of land, sure. But it also has a huge house. Probably even bigger than mine. But I've never been to Bandleman's Estate before, so I can't be sure."

"Bannerman's," Jessica corrected her automatically. "Only, Lila—" She scratched her head. "Are you, like, sure about this?" She hadn't heard anything about a huge house, but then again, she had dozed off while Mr. Clark, the school principal, had talked about the trip at assembly. Maybe she'd missed the part about the house?

"Bandleman, Bangermen, whatever," Lila said airily. "Anyway, I've been in estates like that before, when I was skiing in Switzerland, the summer we spent in the south of France, and when we went to visit friends near Dallas, and they are so unbelievably amazing! They have hot tubs in every room, and an Olympic-size pool in the basement, and a massage person if you want, and you get a whole box of chocolates on your pillow every single night." She looked off into space. "I just can't figure out how the school could rent something like that for the week."

Jessica felt her heart begin to quicken. Things were really looking up. If what Lila said was true, the trip wouldn't just be fun—it would be incredible!

"And the chandeliers!" Lila went on dreamily. "There was this really awesome one on the estate we stayed at in South America. Maybe they have one at Birmingham's. And of course it's fancy dress after five o'clock. Do you have anything suitable?" She turned to Jessica, frowning. "Well, if you don't, you can borrow something from me, even if I am a size or two smaller than you. It'll be white tie and tails for the guys at dinner. I'm looking forward to seeing Bruce Patman in tails, aren't you?" She flashed Jessica a cat-that-ate-the-canary smile.

Jessica could just see Bruce surfing down the banisters of the old Bannerman house in a white suit. Camp was sounding better and better. "And here I thought we were going to be sleeping out under the stars and stuff like that!" she said with a grin.

"Ugh," Lila remarked. "Disgusto. I mean, why would anybody want to do a thing like that?"

Elizabeth Wakefield gently ran her fingers through her long blond hair as she sat at her desk. Outside, the day was beautiful and sunny—exactly the kind of morning she loved best.

She hunched over a piece of paper. "Let's see,"

she muttered to herself. "*Estate* rhymes with—um—"

Wait, Elizabeth told herself. But *wait* didn't seem to fit in the sentence. She scowled and tapped her pencil against the edge of the desk. *What else? Estate, wait, plate, freight. Blate.* Was there any such word as *blate?* Elizabeth wrinkled her nose. She didn't think so.

Elizabeth stared down at the paper in front of her. "We're going camping at Bannerman's Estate," she read aloud. "*We're* going *camp*-ing at *Ban*-ner-man's es-*tate,*" she read again, making sure it was in proper rhythm. "I *know* I'll have *fun* and—"

And what? Elizabeth strained to think. "I know I'll have fun, and I'll maybe eat a plate," she murmured. *No. Too stupid. A plate of what?* "I know I'll have fun since my clothes will be on straight." *Gag!*

Elizabeth rolled her eyes. *What else rhymes with* estate? *Estate. Plate, wait, eight, gate, hate, great—*

Great!

"*We're* going *camp*-ing at *Ban*-nerman's es-*tate!*" Elizabeth chanted, suddenly excited. "I *know* I'll have *fun,* and I *know* it will be *great!*" Her pencil scratched across the page.

Now the words were coming so fast, her hand could hardly keep up. "We'll all go canoeing, and we'll sit out in the breeze," Elizabeth whispered as her pencil flew. "We'll have campfires and marshmallows and even climb some trees." She crossed the *T* with a flourish and went on to the next line. "We'll be sleeping out in tents, underneath the stars."

Elizabeth could see herself out on a beautiful night, looking at the dazzling array of stars overhead. It would be like a whole bunch of fireworks going off all at the same time, only better.

"We'll be sleeping out in tents, underneath the stars," Elizabeth repeated, her lips curling into a smile. "We'll be walking, maybe running, and we'll never ride in cars." Well, that last line was kind of lame, but she could always work on it later.

What else? "We'll see deer and moose and eagles, and maybe a bear." Elizabeth didn't really expect bears, but that was one of the things that made camping exciting, wasn't it? You never knew exactly what might happen. "And if it rains once or twice, we won't even care." *No. Scratch that.* "We *just* won't even care."

Now for the hard part. Elizabeth suddenly realized that her heart was thumping. Did she dare or didn't she? "And then there is this certain boy," she wrote quickly before she could stop herself.

She frowned at the paper. The face of Todd Wilkins, Elizabeth's sort-of boyfriend, floated in her mind. Todd was cute and fun to be with. But did she really want to, you know, write about him in this poem? "And then there is this certain boy," she repeated under her breath. . . .

No. Too dangerous. What if her brother, Steven, read it accidentally on purpose? He'd pick on her for the next sixty years. She shuddered as she thought about her devoted brother saying in a silly voice,

"Oh, my! Where did I put this certain boy?" or "Oh, Elizabeth, why don't you write a letter to a certain boy?" or even worse, "Telephone, Elizabeth! I think it's your *certain boy* (wink, wink, snicker, snicker)."

No, that would be too much to deal with. Reluctantly Elizabeth erased the line. She sighed. It was too bad. Going to camp with the whole middle school would be fun, that was for sure. But she had really been looking forward to spending some time with Todd.

She smiled and gazed off into the brilliant sunshine. She could see them now, just the two of them together, strolling hand in hand down the paths at Bannerman's Estate. Or even standing under the full moon and the starlit sky. *Yes.* Elizabeth's throat tightened as she thought of Todd staring up into the sky and squeezing her hand. They'd turn to look at each other, and they'd smile, and . . .

Elizabeth swallowed hard. No, Todd had to be in the poem somehow. She'd just have to figure out a good way to hide what she'd written, that was all. Before she could stop herself, she seized the pencil and started writing.

"But best of all is this handsome guy," Elizabeth barely whispered, just in case her brother was lurking outside the door. "His name is Todd and—"

Was that a noise? She froze and listened intently.

"Hello?" she called out softly after a moment.

No answer.

Just nerves, Elizabeth told herself, sucking in her

breath. *Jessica and Lila are downstairs, and Steven is I don't know where, and anyway, they have better things to do than to spy on me.* But she erased "His name is Todd," just to be on the safe side. Maybe his name shouldn't come into it.

With siblings like hers, you couldn't be too careful.

Two

◇

"There you are!" Jessica said happily once she had flung open the door to Elizabeth's room. "Hey, listen to what Lila just told me! It's so awesome, you're not going to believe it!"

"But it's true," Lila added, following Jessica. She gave a heavy sigh and looked around Elizabeth's bedroom. "Is this really the decorating style you want, Elizabeth? It's so—so old-fashioned. Everyone's into purple and yellow nowadays."

"That wasn't what we meant to say," Jessica added hastily. While she secretly agreed that Elizabeth's taste wasn't always the best, she didn't like it when her friends started in on her sister. After all, that was *her* job. "We were going to say—" She paused and stared closely at her twin. "Hey, what are you doing anyway?"

Elizabeth draped herself across her desk, knocking a pencil to the floor. "None of your business," she said. "Next time could you knock before you barge into my room?"

"Huh?" Jessica looked to the door and back. "Knock?"

"Oh, never mind!" Elizabeth rolled her eyes. "But as long as you're here, I've been meaning to ask you something. Next Saturday is April Fools' Day. Did you want to do our usual switcheroo this year?" Every April Fools' Day for as long as they could remember, the twins had changed identities. They'd gone to each other's classes, hung out with each other's friends, and even tried to fool their own families.

Jessica made a face. "Well, to tell you the honest truth, Lizzie, I think we're way too mature for that this year," she said. *At least I am,* she thought. "I mean, it was fine back when we were, like, third-graders. But we're *twelve* now."

Elizabeth smiled briefly. "That's kind of what I thought," she admitted. "I was feeling the same way."

"Then that's settled," Jessica said quickly. She *was* too mature to do something dumb like pretending she was Elizabeth. Anyway, much as she loved her sister, she was quite sure that being Jessica was a lot more interesting. "So listen to this. What's Bannerman's Estate like? In your own words, I mean."

"Bannerman's Estate?" Elizabeth blinked. "Is this some kind of trick question?"

"Oh, of course not!" Lila sounded shocked.

"No way," Jessica lied. "Come on, Lizzie. Describe Bannerman's Estate."

Elizabeth took a deep breath and wiggled her fingers. Jessica thought she could see a sheet of notebook paper creeping out from under Elizabeth's sweater. "Well—," Elizabeth began slowly. "It's like they described it at the assembly, I guess. Pine trees, and hiking trails, and a lake . . ."

"Yeah, right," Lila said scornfully.

"Nope," Jessica said. "Well, I mean, yup. That's part of it. But what else?"

"What *else?*" Elizabeth repeated slowly. "Um—I think they said something about a ropes obstacle course. And, um, a nature museum in an old cabin."

"Good!" Jessica shot back. "Buildings. What other kinds of buildings?" She leaned forward. "Come on, come on," she said excitedly.

"Buildings?" Elizabeth looked blank. "I guess— maybe there's a building for the infirmary. You know, where people go if they're sick. And—" She pulled a little more of the paper out. If she squinted, Jessica could see a couple of words written on the top. "Are we playing charades or something?"

"More like Twenty Questions," Jessica said importantly. "How about this. Where do we sleep?" She peered at Elizabeth's paper. The first word said "We're." Unless it said "We've." Or "Here." It was hard to tell, reading upside down. "So where do we sleep?" she asked again impatiently.

Elizabeth shrugged. "Tents. And sleeping bags."

Gotcha! "No, we don't!" Jessica crowed. "Why do you think it's called Bannerman's *Estate*, huh?"

"What are you talking about?" Elizabeth frowned. "It's an estate because it's got a lot of land. And it used to belong to some people named Bannerman."

"The *house*, Lizzie, the *house*," Jessica said, resisting the impulse to grab her sister by the shoulders and shake some sense into her. "The huge house that the Bannerpeople built?"

"The one that we're going to stay in," Lila added, settling onto Elizabeth's bed. "Elizabeth, I don't know why you're bringing a sleeping bag. Most estates have perfectly adequate blankets, and there aren't any bedbugs, I promise."

"Bedbugs?" Elizabeth scratched her head and looked from Lila to Jessica. "Estates? Houses? What are you two *talking* about?"

"We're staying in an estate," Jessica said, feeling as if she were explaining something to a two-year-old. "Like, a big house? Like, bigger than Lila's, even. With air-conditioning and blow-dryers, OK? So lose the sleeping bag. You don't want to be the only kid in the school who thinks she's going *camping*." She said the last word with the ugliest face she could manage.

"Yeah, Elizabeth," Lila put in. "You don't want to be the only kid in—"

"But we *are* going camping," Elizabeth interrupted.

Trust Elizabeth to always get things wrong. "But we aren't!" Jessica said triumphantly. "Ask Lila. She's been in lots of estates before."

"Tons," Lila added with her nose in the air.

Elizabeth shook her head vehemently. "That's a different kind of estate," she said. "You've got it all wrong."

Lila made a face. "You just don't know, Elizabeth, because you've never been. Now, Bannerville's might not be as fancy as the one I went to in Massachusetts, but—"

Elizabeth sighed. "I think Bannerman's Estate *used* to be like that," she said. "But it isn't anymore. There's just ruins of an old house. That's what they told us at that assembly. Weren't you paying attention?"

Lila put her hands on her hips. "You're just jealous because you haven't been to an estate and I have," she accused Elizabeth.

"Yeah, Elizabeth," Jessica put in. But she was feeling just the slightest twinge of doubt. Elizabeth sounded awfully sure of herself. And though she hated to admit it, Elizabeth was pretty good about getting her facts straight. While Lila—well, Lila wasn't.

"I'll prove it to you," Elizabeth offered, tucking the piece of paper under her sweater. "Didn't you read the information packet they sent home?"

"Information packet?" Jessica dimly remembered that the school had sent home a packet about the trip. She hadn't read it, of course—hadn't even glanced at it. It had looked incredibly boring.

"I've got it right here on my bedside table," Elizabeth said. Quickly she took the paper from under her sweater and lay it facedown on the desk. Crossing the room, Elizabeth grabbed a folder and leafed through it. "Packing sheet . . . recommended reading . . ."

She's probably read all the books on the recommended reading list, Jessica thought bleakly. She could just imagine their titles too. *At Home with Mr. and Mrs. Bannerman. The Incredibly Boring History of a Small California Town. What Life Was Like Before the Railroad, and Why It Was Totally Gross.* "You said you were sure," she hissed angrily to Lila. It was always nice to have somebody else to blame.

Lila frowned worriedly. "Well—well, she doesn't necessarily know what she's talking about," she responded uncertainly.

"Here we are," Elizabeth said, running her finger slowly down a page. "'Information Sheet for Campers . . . please be aware that the Bannerman Estate is highly primitive,'" she read. "'Students should not expect all the comforts of home.'"

Jessica bit her lip and looked accusingly at Lila.

"'For example, there are no televisions, microwaves, or blow-dryers available at the campsites,'" Elizabeth read on, stressing the word *campsites* very slightly.

"That's ridiculous," Lila said from the bed. "Do you realize how many more boxes I'm going to have to pack to take all that stuff along, then? No *way* am I being caught out in the woods without my electric toothbrush and my automatic curling iron and my portable satellite dish and my—"

"'Nor should campers bring such items from home,'" Elizabeth read, "'as there are no electrical outlets in the tents or outbuildings—'"

"Let me see that!" Jessica stepped forward and snatched the sheet out of her sister's hand. "You're making it up!" But even before she scanned the letter, she knew the truth: Elizabeth wasn't making it up.

Only a school administrator could write like that.

"'Please follow these directives,'" Jessica read aloud. "'Also please be aware that while all tents are made from waterproof materials, in heavy storms minor leakage may occur. . . .'" Jessica's voice trailed off. "They're saying we're going to get wet!" she sputtered.

"Not *very* wet," Elizabeth pointed out. "It says 'may' occur, and only in heavy storms—"

But Jessica was too disgusted to listen. A Jacuzzi, chandeliers, queen-size beds piled high with lots of pillows—gone.

Hello, leaky tents and smelly sleeping bags.

She glared at Lila. It was a good thing she actually enjoyed camping and the outdoors.

Mostly.

"I'm sorry, Jessica," Elizabeth said helplessly, setting the folder back on her bedside table. "I didn't realize you thought the trip would be different."

"Oh—that's all right," Jessica said. She leaned back against Elizabeth's desk. "It's not your fault. I guess."

"So what am I going to do in the wilderness for a week?" Lila moaned. She pressed her face into Elizabeth's pillow. "I'd stay home if I could, but Daddy is on a trip to Rangoon, wherever *that* is, and Mrs. Pervis is visiting her sister in San Diego."

Elizabeth bit her lip. Half of her wanted to be sympathetic. It wasn't much fun to expect one thing and then get another. But the other half wanted to tell Lila to grow up and get a life. "It'll be fun," she said, plastering a smile on her face.

Lila sighed. "Oh, yeah," she said mirthlessly. "Loads."

Jessica gave a half grin. "At least," she predicted, "you'll survive it."

"If I can't have my laptop and modem so I can E-mail my dad . . . ," Lila threatened.

"No, really," Elizabeth said. "I'm serious. Camp is going to be so cool. We'll learn all about nature and about the history of the estate—" She broke off as she saw Lila's scowl deepen, remembering that she wasn't talking to someone who exactly appreciated nature and history.

"Canoeing and, um, sunbathing—," Jessica began.

"*If* it ever stops raining," Lila interrupted.

"And volleyball, and walks in the woods, and the smell of flowers," Elizabeth went on. "And clear starry nights, and . . . and roasting marshmallows over a campfire—"

Lila shuddered and turned her back in disgust. "Campfires? No, thanks!" she said. "I'll probably get cinders in my eye."

"Then we'll take you to the hospital," Jessica said with a shrug.

"And—," Elizabeth stopped, realizing that she wasn't getting anywhere. She just couldn't understand why Lila wasn't excited about the trip. She could see herself now, her hand curled inside Todd's as they sat by the campfire, watching the flames crackle and hiss and seeing each other's eyes sparkling in the moonlight while they sang some song that was really pretty and kind of romantic but not mushy or anything, something like "Home on the Range" only with better words. She sniffed the air experimentally. She could practically smell the woodsmoke.

"Hey, what's this anyway?" Jessica asked curiously.

Elizabeth broke out of her daydream. Her heart sank like a stone. "Put that down!" she demanded, running toward her sister and grabbing for the piece of paper in Jessica's hand. The paper with her totally private poem on it! "Put that down!"

"Not till you tell me what it is," Jessica told her, hiding behind the other side of the desk and holding the paper high in the air.

Elizabeth took a deep breath. "Oh—just a, you know, a list," she said brightly, hoping she made a convincing liar. "Just a to-do list of things I, like, need to do! Before we go to camp tomorrow, I mean," she added. "It wouldn't really interest you. So you can put it down now."

Jessica snorted. "You're lying," she said.

"I am not!" To her dismay, Elizabeth could feel her cheeks growing hot.

"Are too." Jessica looked up at the paper. "'We're going camping at Bannerman's Estate,'" she read aloud in a flat voice. "'I know I'll have fun—'"

"Put it down!" Elizabeth pleaded, her heart beating furiously.

"'—And I know it will be great,'" Jessica went on as if Elizabeth had never spoken. She turned her head to stare at her sister. "This is a poem!" she announced, as if Elizabeth didn't already know.

"I said, put it down!" Elizabeth reached across the desk but only managed to knock over her lamp.

"Temper, temper," Jessica scolded her. "Let's see what else. 'We'll all go canoeing, and we'll sit out in the breeze,'" she read.

"*I* won't," Lila said crossly.

"My sister, the human greeting card," Jessica said. "I knew you liked to read this stuff, Lizzie, but I didn't know you *wrote* it too. 'We'll have campfires and marshmallows, and if it rains we'll freeze.'"

"That's not what I wrote," Elizabeth said, clenching her teeth. "*Mine* says—"

"Yeah, but I like my way better," Jessica told her. "'We'll be sleeping out in tents, underneath the stars.' Elizabeth, this is truly pathetic."

"You put that down!" Elizabeth shouted furiously. Scrambling behind her desk, she grabbed Jessica's outstretched arm. "That poem is private, and—"

"Oh, my gosh," Jessica said, breaking free and

dashing for the doorway. "Listen to this, Lila!"

"What?" Lila sat up on the bed. "Is it about something good, like VCRs?"

"It's, like, almost at the very end," Jessica said, her face breaking into a huge grin. "It says, 'And best of all, the very cutest guy I know / Will walk with me beneath the stars, and we'll walk slow.'" She whistled. "Elizabeth Wakefield! Who's the lucky guy? As if I didn't know."

"Probably that boring old Todd Wilkins." Lila came over to look.

Elizabeth could tell she was losing control. "Number one," she said, her eyes flashing, "Todd's not boring. And number two, that's only a rough draft. And number three—" She snatched the paper from Jessica's hand. "Number three, you have no right to read my private writings!"

"Well, you shouldn't have left it where I could see it," Jessica said.

"It was on *my* desk!" Elizabeth sputtered. "And *you* were the one who barged in here and just plain—" She let her hands fall, the poem safely in her grip. "Get out of here now!" she threatened, stamping her foot. "Or I'll—" She didn't know what she'd do, but she was angry enough to do it, whatever it was.

"OK, OK," Jessica said, backing away in mock surrender. "You win. Sorry." She turned and dashed for the stairs. "And don't worry," she called back over her shoulder, "I won't tell Todd!"

"Me either," Lila said. "Hey, Elizabeth, what about pasta machines? Do you think they'd let me bring one? It doesn't take up much space and—"

"*Out*," Elizabeth hissed, and she slammed the door. Taking a deep breath, she looked at her poem again. Jessica's fingernails had left impressions all over the paper. She considered throwing it away. "'We'll paddle together all over the lake,'" she muttered, staring at the last two lines—the two lines that Jessica hadn't read. "'And we'll sit and hold hands; make no mistake.'"

Actually the poem isn't bad at all, she told herself. She closed her eyes and rested against the door. It didn't make any sense to let Jessica spoil her entire week, did it? Her thoughts drifted off to Todd once more: Elizabeth holding her head up high and ignoring Jessica's taunts, Elizabeth and Todd floating together in a canoe across a lake of bright blue water, Elizabeth staring deeply into Todd's eyes . . .

Elizabeth's eyes opened suddenly. Well, what did she have to lose anyway? Crossing back to her desk, she grabbed her pencil and scribbled two more lines to close the poem.

"And maybe, just maybe, this young mister and miss," she said softly, her heart beginning to soar again, "will take a quick moment and might even kiss!"

Elizabeth set the pencil down with a sigh.

The magic of the trip was back.

*   *   *

Jessica brushed her teeth thoughtfully Saturday night. Tomorrow they'd leave for camp. She was all packed, except for the dozens of things she knew she'd need but couldn't have: mousetraps, bear repellent, and all the stores at Sweet Valley Mall.

It was funny. First she'd been excited about going. Then Lila had told her about the fancy estates, and she'd *really* been excited—until Elizabeth had exploded that idea. Now she was excited again, but she couldn't help thinking about all the stuff she wouldn't be able to bring along.

"Aren't you done in there yet?" Elizabeth called into the bathroom.

Jessica made a noise that she hoped sounded like, "No." Elizabeth hadn't been very nice to her all afternoon. She supposed it was because she'd read her sister's poem. It wasn't that bad a poem actually, and Jessica couldn't see why Elizabeth had gotten so upset about it. *After all,* she told herself, *if she'd really wanted me not to read it, she'd have kept it hidden.*

A picture flashed into Jessica's mind: Elizabeth and Todd strolling together hand in hand. What was it her sister had written? *"Walk beneath the starry skies and walk real slow?"* Something like that anyway. Jessica had to admit, her sister had a way with words. She could practically see the two of them, surrounded by huge pine trees, the beam of a flashlight bobbing along in the darkness. . . .

It wasn't a bad picture at all. Especially not if

she replaced Elizabeth with herself and Todd with her own sort-of boyfriend, Aaron Dallas.

There would be owls and crickets and a full moon, but no snakes or mosquitoes or anything disgusting like that. And there would be no one anywhere around, just the two of them in the wilderness.

Come to think of it, she'd never been kissed before. The woods might just be a perfect place for the first one.

Maybe this trip would be even better than she'd expected.

Elizabeth rapped on the door. "Come on, Jessica!" she snapped. "Get a move on, OK?"

Jessica sprang to life. "Sure, Lizzie," she sang out, wiping her hands and opening the door to her own room. "And thanks!"

"Thanks? Thanks for what?" Elizabeth grumbled as she came into the bathroom.

But Jessica was already gone.

Three

◇

"At ze Bannerman Estate things are strange," Winston Egbert said in a spooky voice. "On ze night of ze full moon ze ghost of Mees-tair Bannerman walks!"

Elizabeth sighed. The bus ride was only ten minutes old, and already she was getting just a little tired of Winston's antics. "Hey, guys, let's sing," she suggested, looking around.

"And eef you get too close," Winston went on, "he shoooots out his claws, and zey are like ice!"

Todd grinned wryly. He was seated just across the aisle. "Yeah, let's," he agreed. "Ah-one, ah-two, ah-Take me out to the ball game . . ."

"Take me out to the crowd!" Elizabeth joined in, winking at her friend Amy Sutton, who was sitting next to her.

"And zen he clouts you over ze head with a baseball bat," Winston shouted above the noise of the singers. "And he picks up your brains with a mitt and—"

"Hey, quiet down up there!" a voice from the back of the bus shouted. "*Some* of us are trying to get our beauty sleep!"

Elizabeth turned to look. It was Janet Howell, one of Jessica's friends. She was an eighth-grader and president of the Unicorn Club—and in Elizabeth's opinion one of the snobbiest girls in school. *She wouldn't mind if we were singing Johnny Buck songs*, Elizabeth told herself, amused. *It isn't the noise that bugs her—our song just isn't cool enough.* She decided to sing extraloud just to annoy Janet. "I don't care if I never get back," she sang at the top of her voice.

"And *zen*," Winston went on dramatically, "ze ghost of Mees-tair Bannerman jumps out and says, 'Tag! You're it!'"

"Wait a minute." Randy Mason pressed his fingers to his forehead. "He does that *after* he pulls out your brains? Why don't I believe you, Winston?"

"Ah," Winston said, wiggling his fingers. "Zat is because you are an idiot. Only idiots do not believe ze great storyteller Winston Egbert."

"At the old—ball—game!" Amy, Todd, and Elizabeth finished.

"*Quiet!*" Janet bellowed.

Gently Elizabeth reached across the aisle and squeezed Todd's hand. "This is going to be such a cool trip," she said.

Todd's eyes met hers. "Don't I know it."

"I bet there'll be lots of nice walks a person could take," Elizabeth said casually. "If they wanted to be, like, alone for a few minutes."

Todd nodded slowly. "Maybe a trail that leads to, say, a quiet stream."

"And rocks where the person could eat a snack," Elizabeth suggested. She could almost feel the cool sparkling water against her toes. "They might even take, you know, a friend along," she said, not daring to look Todd directly in the eye.

Todd bit his lip. "I—guess they could," he agreed after a moment. "If the trail was, like, big enough for two. And if they brought a . . . you know. A big enough snack."

Elizabeth's heart soared. "Well, if you—um, see a place like that anywhere, maybe you could let me know!" she said brightly.

Todd nodded. "And the same for you, OK?"

"Come on, guys," Amy said impatiently. "Let's sing some more. How about something really goofy?"

"Like 'Old MacDonald'?" Winston suggested hopefully.

"Yeah!" Todd leaned across the aisle and nudged Elizabeth. "I'd say that's goofy enough."

The perfect song to irritate my sister and her friends, Elizabeth thought. "You bet!" she agreed.

"She's *your* sister, Jessica," Janet pointed out sourly. Jessica sighed. "It was an accident of birth," she said under her breath. It was a line from an old movie she'd seen once when she'd stayed home sick from school. There were times when she couldn't believe that her sister had grown up on the same planet with her, let alone in the same house.

"With a meow, meow here and a meow, meow there," half the bus warbled. Jessica made a face. *Typical Elizabeth.*

Janet stared directly into Jessica's eyes. "So what exactly are you planning to do about it?" she demanded.

Jessica shifted uncomfortably on the hard bus seat. There didn't seem to be much she *could* do about it. Jessica was Jessica, and Elizabeth was Elizabeth, and—well, they didn't have much in common.

"Yeah, Jessica," Lila put in. "What are you going to do about it, huh?"

"*I* happen to think it's a problem if you won't do anything about your sister," Janet went on, her voice rising over the chorus of "With a neigh, neigh here." "What do the *rest* of you think?"

Mouth dry, Jessica looked around at her fellow Unicorns. Ellen Riteman and Kimberly Haver were both frowning. Even Mandy Miller, who usually was pretty nice, didn't exactly have a smile on her face. "Well—I'll talk to her," she said hesitantly.

Janet glanced around the circle of Unicorns clustered in the back of the bus. "That's a start anyway. But it isn't enough. Go sabotage their song."

Sabotage their song? Jessica looked around in

dismay. How in the world was she going to do that? "But Janet—"

Janet folded her arms. "Do it, Jessica."

Biting her lip, Jessica started out of her seat.

She had learned from long experience that arguing with Janet was next to impossible.

"*E-i-e-i-o!*" Elizabeth shouted out. She looked over to Todd and grinned. This was fun. Especially because she could just imagine how much the Unicorns in the back of the bus were enjoying it.

"And then there's the ghost of Mrs. Bannerman," Winston was saying, sticking his nose in the air and talking in an English accent. "The poor lady went shopping one day and fell into a sewer. . . ."

"And on that farm he had—" Elizabeth looked around questioningly. She wasn't sure there were any other farm animals left. "And on that farm?" she supplied, hoping somebody would jump in.

"Penguin," said a voice above her head.

Elizabeth looked up, startled, to see her sister. "What are you doing here, Jessica?" she asked suspiciously.

"Never mind *that*," Jessica snapped. "I have an animal for you. And on that farm there was a penguin. *E-i-e-i-ugh.*"

A penguin? Elizabeth shrugged. "And on that farm there was a penguin, *e-i-e-i-o.*" She thought she heard Jessica chanting "ugh" at the end, but she couldn't be sure. "With a—what sound do penguins make anyway?" she asked.

"Urk," Winston stated positively.

"Cheep, cheep," Amy suggested.

"How about 'worra, worra, worra'?" Todd offered.

"If it's a Pittsburgh Penguin," Randy said, "they say this: *gooooal!*"

Elizabeth smiled. *Of course—a hockey player!* "With a *gooooal* here, and a *gooooal* there!" she sang as loudly as possible. "Here a *gooooal*, there a *gooooal*, everywhere a *gooooal, gooooal!*"

"Old MacDonald had a farm!" Randy, Winston, and Todd bellowed tunelessly. *"E-i-e-i-o!"*

Glancing at her sister, she saw to her delight that Jessica was clutching her ears and making her way back down the aisle of the bus.

"Nice *job*, Jessica," Janet said sarcastically. "I said sabotage, not join in."

"Yeah, nice *job*, Jessica," Ellen Riteman agreed.

"And on that farm they had an octopus!" Randy yelled jubilantly.

"Well—I tried," Jessica said softly. How was she supposed to know that the kids would actually start singing about animals that didn't even live on farms?

"Tell them to put in a bear," Aaron Dallas said, turning around in his seat.

Jessica's heart skipped a beat. She'd forgotten that Aaron was sitting only a couple of rows in front of her. He was so handsome, so—so much fun to be around. She still remembered her little daydream about him last night. Maybe this *would* be the week when she'd get her first kiss. There was an empty seat across the aisle from Aaron, and she got up and sauntered down the aisle toward him.

"Where's she going now, I'd like to know?" Janet asked, but Jessica ignored her. "Hi, Aaron," she said, slipping casually into the empty seat.

"Hey!" Aaron greeted her. "How you doing, Jessica?"

"Um—fine," Jessica said, wondering how she could bring up the subject of true romance in the wilderness. "Hey, um, Aaron?"

"Hey, Jess, what do you bet we see a bear this week?" Aaron asked, his eyes shining. "I've been reading about them. I even rented, like, a documentary. It's so cool! Did you know a mother grizzly can kill a grown man with one swipe of her paw?"

Jessica shook her head. *And I didn't really want to know it either.* "Um, Aaron?" she tried again.

"And Kodiak bears," Aaron went on. "Kodiak bears are the *ultimate* cool. If I was a bear, I'd be a Kodiak. Know why?"

The bus hit a pothole. Jessica lurched forward. "Why?"

"'Cause they're even stronger," Aaron said. "They're, like, the Arnold Weissenhammers of the bears. If a man wrestled with a Kodiak, he wouldn't last a *minute.* He might not even last a *second.* It'd be wham, clunk, aah!, and then they'd have to pick up the pieces." He grinned happily. "Yeah, I bet we see a bear. Maybe two bears."

"Um—I guess maybe we will," Jessica said slowly. "Hey, Aaron, did you know there were lots of quiet trails around the Bannerman Estate?"

"Yeah?" Aaron shrugged. "Are there bears on them? You should check if there are lots of berry bushes on the trails. If the berries get eaten from the top, it's birds. If they get eaten from the bottom, it's *bears*." He smacked his lips. "Hey, if you see any berry bushes that got eaten from the bottom, let me know, OK?"

Jessica sighed. "That's not what I meant, Aaron." Either Aaron was unusually dense today or else . . . she wrinkled her nose. "What I mean is," she added, "some of those trails are, like, you know, kind of private?"

Aaron gave her a funny look. "You mean, they belong to somebody else? Then you couldn't walk on them anyway." He made a face. "Bummer."

"That isn't what I meant either!" Jessica was beginning to feel exasperated. First Elizabeth. Then Janet. Now Aaron. What was this anyway—Give Jessica a Hard Time Week? "I mean, a trail where a guy and a girl could walk together. *Alone* together," she added in case he still didn't get it. "You know—hand in hand beneath the stars?"

She held her breath, waiting for his response.

"Hand in *hand?*" Aaron asked incredulously. "Beneath the *stars?* You're kidding, right? Who'd want to do a thing like that?"

"I thought—," Jessica began. Her heart

hammered. Quickly she forced a smile onto her face. "Well, um, some people might think it was pretty cool. I'm not saying who, exactly, but I heard that, um, *some* people might . . . like . . . doing that." She swallowed hard.

Aaron snorted. "Not *me*, kid. I'll be too busy hunting for bears."

"Oh." Jessica bit her lip. "Oh. I—I see." Standing up quickly, she narrowly avoided being thrown into Aaron's lap as the bus swerved to the side. *The nerve!* she thought, clenching and unclenching her fists. He just didn't get it. Well, forget about him, then. She went back to her seat and slid in next to Ellen.

"What's *your* problem?" Ellen asked.

"Oh—nothing," Jessica lied. *I hope one of those Kodiak bears eats him alive,* she thought, feeling only a little better. She could just see Aaron in a boxing ring with the biggest bear in the world, Aaron screaming as the bear came at him with a gleam in its eye, Aaron lying on the floor screaming for mercy as the bear descended on him with open claws and hungry jaws, roaring as it tore apart his tender flesh. . . .

At least until he agreed that maybe it would be pretty cool to go for a long walk in the woods with Jessica.

Four

◇

This is perfect, Elizabeth thought that night. *It must be what heaven is like!*

She was in her sleeping bag at Bannerman's Estate, curled up next to Amy and four other kids in a supersize tent. All around were the sounds of nature. Elizabeth could hear the wind whistling through the trees. There were crickets chirping in the distance and frogs ribbiting in a pond. An owl hooted somewhere near the boys' side of the camp. Elizabeth stretched, a smile on her face. Through the mosquito netting of the tent's entrance she caught a glimpse of a few brilliant stars, which lit up the sky much more than they ever did in Sweet Valley.

She felt radiant.

Elizabeth filled her lungs with the cool, pure mountain air. Somewhere in the darkness a stream burbled.

That's the stream Todd and I will walk along this week, she promised herself. *Alone together, just us two, under the trees and the sky.*

Closing her eyes, Elizabeth smiled and rolled over. This just might be the best week she would ever have.

"I don't get it," Ellen said. "How do they expect me not to watch *Hunky Lifeguards* on TV? Did they forget it was Sunday or something? I mean, hello?"

The Unicorns were all clustered together in a tent near Elizabeth's, and not one of them was close to going to sleep. "You'd think they'd at least give us a TV just for the night," Jessica added. "I mean, we're not just missing *Hunky Lifeguards* but *Totally Cool Home Videos* too."

"And *Fatal Illness,*" Kimberly added darkly. "Did you see that episode where the really hot doctor wanted to marry the nurse, only she was really his long-lost sister in disguise? And then he died of chicken pox or something? That was *so* cool."

"This place is a joke," Lila said from the darkness. "I've wiggled and wiggled and I can't get to sleep, and I'm getting eaten alive by bugs. I want to go home."

"Lila! That kind of attitude reflects badly on the club," Janet said disapprovingly. "What's the matter? You can't handle a little nature?"

"I like nature just fine," Lila argued. "Only I like it in a cage. Or in a flowerpot. Where I *don't* like nature is when its roots are sticking into my back. I feel like a human pincushion."

"It's just because of your house," Ellen said. "See, you're just too used to all the stuff in your house is all."

"Yeah," Kimberly agreed. "You're too soft. You can't rough it the way the rest of us can."

"Yeah, Lila," Jessica said, anxious to get back into the club's good graces. But she couldn't help being suddenly aware of a large root sticking into her own back.

"I don't even have an air conditioner," Lila said sadly. "Here we are, out in the middle of nowhere, and I don't have an air conditioner. How am I supposed to survive for a whole week without an air conditioner—will somebody tell me that?"

"It's not the end of the world, Lila," Kimberly said dismissively. "Of course," she added after a moment, "an air conditioner *would* be kind of nice."

"And there are kind of a lot of bugs," Ellen said. She wrinkled her nose. "Not that I'm complaining, exactly. But there are kind of a lot of them."

Jessica moved uncomfortably. She hoped a spider wouldn't spin a web across her face in the middle of the night.

"And you'd think somebody in charge could tell those crickets to shut up," Janet grumbled. "Of course, they aren't really *bothering* me or anything. I'm not soft, the way Lila is."

"And the roots aren't all *that* bad," Jessica said

bravely. "I don't know about anybody else, but I'm planning to have a great time this week." She swallowed hard. "A *great* time," she repeated when nobody else chimed in. *Even if the roots are shaped like little tiny daggers.*

Lila sat up. "*My* roots are stabbing me in the back. But I can't sit up all night. It would just utterly destroy my posture."

"Anyway," Mandy said, "if you were sitting up and a bear came into the tent, it'd grab you first."

With a little scream Lila lay back down.

Bears. Jessica sighed again, remembering how obnoxious Aaron had been to her. She twisted and turned, trying to find a sort-of comfortable position. Every breath brought in the odor of grass and leaves and—if she smelled very hard—the faint aroma of skunks, not to mention moose droppings. Or at least what she thought moose dropping probably smelled like.

Plus, it smelled like rain. And the roof of the tent looked about as strong as—as a couple of tissues.

"What was that noise?" Lila's frightened voice floated up to her ears.

"Probably a bear," Janet said gloomily.

"No, it was just the wind in the trees," Mandy said. "I think."

Jessica buried her head in her pillow, which already smelled like the forest. She hoped it wouldn't rain. It wouldn't be very nice to wake up tomorrow floating in a sea of rainwater. Assuming that her sleeping bag floated.

She decided she'd rather not find out.

In the boys' camp on the opposite side of Bannerman Estate, Aaron sat bolt upright, the luminous dial of his wristwatch glowing in the dim moonlight. *Two-thirty. Perfect.* "Wasn't that—a bear?" he half whispered.

No one budged. Todd Wilkins dozed on. Bruce Patman was still snoring. Everyone else seemed to be asleep too.

Aaron's eyes twinkled in the near darkness. One . . . two . . . three . . .

"A bear!" Aaron shouted suddenly, kicking his way out of his sleeping bag. "Look out, everybody!" He hoped he'd gotten exactly the right note of panic into his voice. "It's a bear!"

"A—a what?" Todd's eyes opened slowly. "What—time is it anyway?"

"Quarter past a bear, I mean, I don't know! There's a bear!" Aaron screamed, pointing a trembling forefinger toward the moon. "Help, help, help!"

"A *bear?*" Todd's eyes grew wide. Turning, he shook Bruce roughly. "Hey, Patman, wake up. We've got major trouble here!"

"Save me, save me!" Winston Egbert wailed. "I don't *like* bears! I'm allergic to bears! I'm not allowed to play with bears!" Dressed only in a pair of polka-dotted boxer shorts, Winston plunged through the tent entrance without unzipping the mosquito netting. There was a sickening tearing sound.

Aaron grinned. This was working just fine. "It was *big!*" he insisted. "Huge! Its eyes glowed like . . . like . . . monsters' eyes!" He buried his head in his hands. "It . . . it just stood out there, and then it—it growled."

"Patman!" Todd bawled in Bruce's ear. "Get out while the getting's good! Bear alert!"

Aaron took a quick look around. All around him kids were squealing, screaming, and heading for the hills.

"We should look for footprints," Randy Mason said doubtfully.

No, we shouldn't, you little twerp, Aaron thought. "No time for that!" he argued. "It may still be out there. Shift into overdrive!"

"What's the problem? Aliens landing?" With a gigantic yawn Bruce sat up and stretched.

"A bear!" Todd said. "Hit the road!"

"A *bear?*" Bruce reached under his pillow and pulled out a pocketknife. "Where?" He stepped out of his sleeping bag and flailed madly around with the knife. "Just show me where he is!"

"Wait!" Aaron reached for Bruce's wrist—but he was too late. The knife's blade pierced the roof of the tent and slashed up into the sky.

"Run!" Aaron shouted, half pushing Bruce out the tent. Outside he could hear the hubbub of what sounded like a million voices. Lights flashed. Feet pounded.

It worked, Aaron told himself, a small grin breaking out on his face. Sticking his head up through the ruined remains of the canopy, he stared out at the scene. There were kids sobbing, kids screaming, kids running in circles. Kids clutching backpacks and heavy jackets, kids shivering in underpants and bare feet. Kids looking around nervously, hoping that the bear wasn't coming at them from behind.

It was a truly awesome sight. Aaron couldn't help himself. The small grin became a big grin, and the big grin became a laugh, and—quickly he ducked back into the tent.

"Hey!"

Aaron froze. The voice belonged to a seventh-grader named Dennis Asher, who was new to Sweet Valley. "Oh, hi, Dennis," he said. "Why aren't you running? Don't you know there's a bear around?"

"Yeah, right." Dennis narrowed his eyes. "There's no bear, and you know it," he charged. "You wouldn't be smiling if there was."

Aaron considered denying it, but he decided not to. He wasn't sure he could pull the wool over Dennis's eyes. Anyway, he wanted the glory. "Yeah," he admitted with a grin. "I thought we needed a little excitement around here."

"Cute, Dallas." Dennis shook his head. "Now what? Are you going up into the mountains to bring back ol' Winston?"

Aaron felt just a twinge of guilt. "Well—no," he said. "And anyway, I didn't exactly make up the whole thing. Not really. I . . . I heard a little noise in the bushes, see, and, um, I kind of jumped to conclusions, know what I mean?" He smirked. "I thought it was a bear. For a minute at least."

Dennis stared at the damaged ceiling. "Yeah," he said after a moment. "Well, listen, Dallas. First, I suggest you go out and tell those kids you, um, jumped to conclusions. Then maybe you'd better put your sleeping bag under that hole. Just in case it rains, you know."

Aaron grinned and nodded.

Even if it rained buckets for the rest of the night. Even if he got into big, *big* trouble. Even if they never found Egbert up there among the mountain lions. His little joke was definitely, definitely worth it.

Five

◇

Jessica was lying on a bed of nails. Every way she turned, sharp points poked into her body. Someone had turned the air conditioner up way too high—she was so cold, she could hardly move. In the distance a dying cow was wheezing terribly.

A whip cracked. "You'll lie on this bed of nails and you'll like it!" a demented voice screeched.

"No! Please, no!" Jessica begged, but the voice paid no attention. Jessica gasped for breath. A zillion mosquitoes swarmed into her throat. Terror rose inside her. Sputtering, she sat up, rubbed her eyes—

And realized that she was in her tent, halfway out of her sleeping bag.

Jessica blinked until the world came into focus. *So it was only a dream,* she thought. Still, every muscle in her body hurt, and a particularly sharp root was digging into her thigh. The day was clear and cold, but Jessica thought she could smell rain. Not to mention a few skunks. She swallowed experimentally. *Good. No mosquitoes.*

"What—time is it?" Kimberly asked in a zombie voice.

"Six-thirty." Ellen yawned. "*Way* too early to be awake."

Jessica lay back down. There was a strange noise in the background. It was a little like a bulldozer, except it wasn't as loud and once in a while you could almost make out a musical note. "Does anybody else hear that awful noise or is it just me?" she asked. Her eyes fluttered shut.

"It's Charlie Cashman," Ellen said sleepily.

"Charlie?" Janet asked incredulously. "What's he doing? Snoring?"

Ellen sighed. "Don't you remember? They told him to bring his trumpet so he could play wake-up call for us every morning."

"Well, somebody ought to give him lessons," Jessica said irritably. "He sounds like a hippopotamus singing opera." She scrunched deeper into her sleeping bag, trying to get warm. "I wish he'd shut up. Doesn't he realize he's disturbing everybody's sleep?"

"Just ignore him." Kimberly curled into a tighter ball.

"Yeah." Ellen yawned. "He'll stop . . . sooner . . . or later."

"I sure hope so," Jessica muttered. She wasn't a

morning person exactly, and listening to Charlie Cashman wheeze his way through a song wasn't her idea of a great way to begin the day. She pressed her hands against her ears. "Want to bet that he's playing mostly wrong notes?" she said, fighting back a yawn.

There was no answer.

Jessica turned her head left and right. All around her lay Unicorns, eyes closed, wrapped in sleeping bags like mummies.

"Up and at 'em!" a man's voice shouted from outside the tent. "Time's a-wasting! Two hours late and forty miles to go!"

Jessica wondered if she should get up like the man was saying. She suspected she probably should.

I'll just—give it a couple more minutes, she thought, her brain feeling thick. After all, it was way too early in the morning to expect anybody to get up right away. *Just a couple—more—minutes—*

Slowly Jessica's elbow bent. Her body slid back to the ground.

And then—I'll get—

Up . . .

"This is the life!" Elizabeth said, carrying a plate piled high with pancakes, blueberries, and sausages to a picnic table near the kitchen. "I already have a huge appetite, and I haven't even done anything yet!"

"I know what you mean," Amy said, digging

her fork into her own breakfast. "There's something about the outdoors that makes you hungry."

"And makes the food taste better," Todd added. "Elizabeth, you look great."

"I do?" Elizabeth tried not to smile too broadly. She patted her hair. "I guess the fresh air agrees with me."

"Well, your cheeks sure look redder than usual," Todd said seriously. "And it doesn't look like you just crawled out of a sleeping bag."

"Yeah, admit it, Elizabeth," Amy said with a laugh. "What'd you do—check into a hotel last night after I fell asleep?"

Elizabeth grinned. "I got up a little early so I'd have time to brush my hair, that's all," she said. She spooned blueberries delicately into her mouth. "Mmm. Perfection!"

"I don't know how they get the sky so blue around here," Amy remarked.

"I know what you mean." Elizabeth breathed deeply. "It's like the air's been scrubbed."

"What did they use?" Todd asked. "Sponges? Or a mop?"

Elizabeth chuckled. She felt terrific. She'd woken up very early that morning during a sudden storm and lain awake for about twenty minutes just listening to the pitter-patter of raindrops on the roof of the tent. It had been a wonderful sound— friendly, cheerful, and somehow soothing. Eventually she'd drifted back to sleep, and when she'd woken for good, the sun was peeking over the horizon and the sky was a brilliant blue.

"Which kind of syrup did you try?" Todd wanted to know. He took a bite of pancake.

"Raspberry." Amy's eyes sparkled. "It's awesome!"

"I'm having the honey nut," Elizabeth said, licking her lips. "I figure I can try one every day as long as we're here."

Todd chewed. "Well, I couldn't wait that long. So I chose two different kinds." He grinned at Elizabeth. "Honey nut, like you, and pineapple."

"Jessica would probably like that kind," Elizabeth mused. Her sister was a sucker for anything pineapple—pineapple juice, pineapple soda, pineapple pizza. Elizabeth shuddered at the thought. There was no accounting for taste. "Speaking of Jessica—where is she?"

"Probably somewhere," Amy said casually. "It's not like we can see everyone who's here right now."

Elizabeth nodded. There were tons of picnic tables all over the campground. But it was also true that it was only seven o'clock, and Jessica wasn't what you would call an early riser.

Well, if Jessica missed breakfast, that was Jessica's problem. Elizabeth cut off a slice of sausage and chewed slowly, relishing the flavor of the meat.

She smiled to herself.

Less than twenty-four hours into the trip, and she was already having the time of her life.

"What do you mean we've missed breakfast?" Janet demanded.

Jessica sat up straight in her sleeping bag. She wasn't cold or tired anymore, but her back hurt. So did her arms. Not to mention her legs, neck, and toes. In fact, her whole body was in major pain. "What's this about breakfast?" she demanded, suddenly aware that she was practically starving to death too.

"Your *sister*," Janet said, tearing off the words as if they were made of paper, "is telling us that we've all overslept. I mean, it's only eight-thirty, for goodness' sake."

"I noticed that you guys weren't at breakfast this morning," Elizabeth said, sounding a little embarrassed. "And when I didn't see you at the assembly either, I thought I'd better—you know, check on you."

"There's good news and bad news." Kimberly yawned. "The bad news is, we missed breakfast. The good news is, we missed assembly."

"Well, actually," Elizabeth said with a frown, "assembly was really cool. A park ranger told us all about the natural world around here. The deer and the owls and the beavers and—"

"Like I said," Kimberly observed pointedly from her sleeping bag.

Elizabeth rolled her eyes. "OK, OK," she said quickly. "But there's more. We all signed up for afternoon classes after the assembly was over. And I think there's only one class left."

"Don't tell me," Jessica said, rubbing her eyes. Not only was she injured all over and starving too, but her eyes wouldn't stay open properly. "It's Mrs. Arnette's."

Elizabeth bit her lip. "Yeah," she admitted. "She'll be talking about history. You know, the whole history of Bannerman's Estate, starting, like, when it was first built?"

"Chills, thrills, and excitement," Jessica grumbled. She reached up to pat her head, realizing to her dismay that her hair was a total mess.

"Like, I just can't wait to be a part of that," Lila said thickly.

"Oh, come on!" Elizabeth smiled. "It'll be fun."

Jessica groaned and covered her face. *Sisters.* Elizabeth was just plain weird, that was all there was to it. She could see her sister in the nursing home at age one hundred and ten, chirping about the beautiful sunrise that she could almost see with her new high-powered trifocals and how she'd gummed down three soft-boiled eggs at breakfast and why hadn't Jessica been there to enjoy it?

"What happened anyway? Didn't you hear Charlie?" Elizabeth asked.

"Oh, we heard Charlie, all right." Ellen sat up slowly and moaned. "Unless it was a water buffalo in serious pain. One or the other."

"So you didn't know he was waking us up?" Elizabeth looked from one Unicorn to the next, her brows furrowed.

Jessica rubbed her aching neck. "Of *course* we knew that," she snapped, wishing a hole would open up and swallow her too-perky-for-her-own-good sister.

"Oh." Elizabeth looked confused. "Then why didn't you get up?"

"At six-thirty in the morning?" Lila asked incredulously.

Elizabeth swallowed. "Doesn't the early morning fresh air make you *want* to get up out of bed?"

"To tell you the honest truth," Janet said, fixing Elizabeth with a look, "it makes us *want* to barf."

Slowly Jessica wiggled out of her sleeping bag. "I guess we'd probably better get going," she said doubtfully, trying to ignore the hunger in her stomach.

"Why bother?" Ellen murmured. "I mean, it's not like anybody cares."

Kimberly yawned. "I'll sit here until they make me get out of the tent."

"But—but how about taking a shower?" Jessica asked uncertainly. "And doing our hair?"

"Well, you could certainly use a shower," Janet said. "Unless you *like* showing Aaron how you look after a night in the woods." She made the word *woods* sound diseased.

"Me? How *I* look?" Jessica's hands flew to her face and hair. "What's wrong with the way I look?"

Quickly she glanced around the tent, and for the first time she actually looked at each of her friends' faces. *Gross.* Her heart sank. If she looked anything like any of them, she was in bad shape. Ellen's hair was a total tangle. Janet's face was streaked with mud. Mandy had grass stains on her left cheek, and Kimberly looked bleary-eyed, as if she were allergic to the whole outdoors. And as for *Lila* . . .

Jessica frowned. The only person who looked even halfway decent was Elizabeth. Who looked more than *halfway* decent, she had to admit.

Just the kind of luck Elizabeth *would* get.

"Yeah, Jessica," Ellen put in. "You look like a steam-roller drove across your face. Or a station wagon."

"I do not!" Jessica shot back. But she was afraid that she probably did. *Great,* she thought gloomily. *I came here planning to get kissed, and now look at me. The grossest girl in camp.*

"But how can you even think about taking a shower, Jessica? Have you smelled the water they have here?" Kimberly held her nose and waved away an imaginary smell. "Pee-you!"

"It majorly stinks," Lila agreed. "You could scrub and scrub and scrub with, like, fifty different shampoos and body lotions, and you'd never get the smell out."

"It's got sulfur in it," Mandy explained. "So it smells like rotten eggs."

Jessica scratched a mosquito bite on her chin. Now that she thought about it, there *had* been something smelly about the water they'd gotten out of the pumps last night. So a shower was out of the question. Washing in filth. *Disgusto.*

On the other hand, she reminded herself, not taking a shower for an entire week was pretty darn disgusto too.

Jessica sighed deeply. "And this trip was sup-posed to be *fun,*" she muttered to no one in particular.

Six

$$\diamondsuit$$

"So, um, do you want to maybe do some stuff?" Elizabeth asked Todd shyly. "Like, together?"

The kids had all morning to explore the camp before lunch and afternoon activities.

Todd nodded. "We could. That might be kind of fun. Um—is there anything you especially wanted to do?"

Elizabeth really wanted to go for a quiet, romantic walk, but she wasn't quite ready to say so out loud. She shrugged and blinked a couple of times. "Oh, I don't much care. Whatever!" she said brightly.

They were standing in the middle of a clump of trees. Elizabeth reflected on all the things they could do: volleyball, swimming, nature walks, checking out the little museum . . . she couldn't imagine how she'd ever be able to get to them all.

Todd moved a step closer to her. "Oh, I don't know," he said. "We could, um, play volleyball, or if you wanted to do something else we could do that instead."

Elizabeth considered. Playing volleyball wouldn't be a very private thing to do. They'd share the court with a lot of other kids, and they might not even be on the same team. . . . "Well, we *could* play volleyball," she said slowly. "Or we could—" She paused.

Todd leaned closer still. His hand was almost on her shoulder. "Could what?"

Elizabeth took a deep breath. She decided to go for it. "Or we could, like, go for a nature walk," she said, pasting on her most brilliant smile.

Todd grinned. A surge of electricity seemed to rush through Elizabeth's body.

"Sure!" he said.

"What happened to *you?*" Jessica asked curiously, staring at Aaron Dallas.

It was later on that morning, and Jessica was leaning against the side of the nature museum. The museum was about the closest thing to civilization the camp had to offer. She'd even spent five minutes or so on the inside—about all she could take of exhibits like "Native Ferns" and "Common Minerals of the Bannerman Estate." The Unicorns had finally left their tent when they'd realized that they had to use the bathroom. Disgusting as the bathroom was, using it was better than the alternatives.

"I said, what happened to you?" Jessica asked when Aaron didn't say anything. He was even more bedraggled than the Unicorns, she decided. He looked like he'd taken an unexpected bath. He also looked like he hadn't gotten an awful lot of sleep.

"Oh, nothing much," Aaron said, studying the ground. "We had a long night over at the boys' camp is all."

"A long night how?" Jessica repeated.

Aaron shrugged. "Oh, some clown woke up in the middle of the night and bugged everybody," he said. "You know Dennis Asher? He's in seventh grade?"

"Not really," Jessica said. She knew him by sight, and that was about it. He was pretty cute, she'd noticed, but she didn't *know* him. "So what'd he do? And how come you look kind of wet?"

Aaron's cheeks reddened. "Well, it was another clown who did that. See, good ol' Bruce Patman was whaling around with this knife, and he chopped this hole in the ceiling of the tent—and then it rained," he finished, staring intently at his fingernails.

"Bruce stabbed the ceiling with a *knife?*" Jessica stepped back in alarm.

"Well, not a *knife* knife," Aaron explained. He stepped a little closer to her. "Just a knife. Like, a pocketknife? Don't worry. *I* was never in any danger."

Jessica shook her head. The boys' camp sounded a little crazy. Suddenly she was very aware of Aaron standing very near her. "Oh," she said awkwardly. "Well, I'm glad you didn't get hurt."

"Only wet," Aaron said. He moved even closer. "And the sleeping bag will dry out. One of these weeks anyway. Hey, Jess, there's something I've been meaning to say to you." Bending forward, he looked her straight in the eye.

Jessica's heart skipped a beat. Aaron must think she didn't look too bad. Maybe he was ready to make up and apologize for the mean things he'd said on the bus. Her fantasy came flooding back— Aaron and Jessica leaning against a tree just like this one, sun shining overhead, his lips puckered to give her her very first kiss. . . .

Jessica breathed deeply. "What is it, Aaron?" she said, fumbling for his hand.

Aaron's gaze flicked to the left. Then his jaw dropped. "A bear!" he screamed, eyes wide. "Run, Jess, run!"

"A bear?" Jessica didn't think twice. She made a mad dash toward the right, away from the museum. The blood pounded in her temples. *A bear!* Maybe she could reach safety. But how could you be safe against a bear? "Do something!" she cried over her shoulder.

"I can't!" Aaron's voice trailed her as she ran.

Jessica's lungs felt close to bursting. She gasped for breath. Climb a tree? But bears could climb faster than humans, couldn't they? Stay on the path? But bears could certainly outrun humans. Her sneakers thudded against the dirt. Quickly she threw herself to the side. Brambles scratched her arms, and one especially long thorny branch pulled across her face as she rolled under a bush. It hurt terribly. But there was no sharp grizzly claw raking across her back and no sharp grizzly teeth aiming hungrily at her head—

Jessica lay still beneath the bush, willing herself to be calm. She couldn't hear footsteps. Had she escaped?

And what had happened to Aaron?

Her heart thumping crazily in her chest, Jessica raised herself onto one elbow and listened hard. A faint trail of blood trickled down her arm, but she scarcely noticed. *I'll give it five seconds*, she decided. *No, ten*. Then she'd get up and make sure the bear wasn't lying in wait for her. *One, one thousand . . . two, one thousand . . . three, one thousand . . .*

Her throat felt incredibly dry.

Four, one thousand, she thought, trying to avoid a sense of panic. She licked her lips and realized she'd lost count. *Better begin all over again. Just in case. One, one thousand . . . two, one thousand—*

What was that?

Jessica held her breath. But it didn't sound like a bear. It sounded like—laughter. Like *Aaron Dallas's* laughter.

But it couldn't be. *Could* it?

"Wow!" Aaron's voice drifted to her hiding place. "Truly awesome! You really fell for it, Jess, didn't you!"

Clenching her fists, Jessica scrambled to her feet. So it was true. "You *jerk!*" she yelled, getting thorns stuck in her hair as she clambered through the bushes. "You complete and total *idiot!* This was all a trick—wasn't it?" She didn't wait for an answer. "You ought to be ashamed of yourself! I've never been so humiliated in my whole life!"

"Sorry," Aaron said with a grin. "I couldn't resist. Oh, man! The look on your face!" He slapped his knee and went off into gales of laughter.

It took all Jessica's self-control not to pulverize Aaron on the spot. "What a . . . what an . . ." She reached deep into her brain for the perfect word. "Of all the incredibly *juvenile* things to be doing—"

Aaron smirked. "It was just a joke," he said. "Can't you take a joke, Jessica? I'm only, like, teasing you."

Teasing! "If that's teasing, then I'm Johnny Buck!" Jessica hissed. "I never want to look at you again. I never want to think about you again!" She broke into a run, her ears still ringing with the sound of Aaron's laughter.

She had truly never been so humiliated. Not ever. Not even once.

"Look at this one," Elizabeth said, bending down along the path. With gentle fingers she pulled a clover off an old stone wall. "It's a four leafer. See?"

She opened the clover and placed it carefully in the palm of her left hand. The four leaves glistened with the morning dampness.

"It's really pretty." Todd leaned close to see. "All the leaves look exactly alike."

"And it's supposed to bring me luck, right?" Elizabeth raised an eyebrow and smiled at Todd.

"Well, that's the story anyway." Todd grinned. "Maybe you should run it as an article in the *Sixers*." Elizabeth was the editor of the *Sweet Valley Sixers*, the sixth-grade newspaper. "I can see the headline now." He stretched out his arms as if he were holding a paper. "Editor Finds Four-Leaf Clover at Camp."

Elizabeth laughed. "You mean, Editor Gets Replaced for Running Stupid Articles."

"That too." Todd winked. "Well, I guess we'll find out the truth about four-leaf clovers. If you have a good week at camp, then they're lucky. Or at least this one was."

"But I wouldn't want to be the only one to get all the luck," Elizabeth said seriously. "I'd . . . feel bad if I got lots of luck and you didn't get any."

Todd flashed her a lopsided smile. "Thanks," he murmured. "But I think I'll be OK. After all, if I find a three leafer and a one leafer, that makes four, doesn't it?"

Elizabeth laughed. "I don't think it works that way, Todd."

Todd's eyes sparkled in the sunlight. "Well, then, how about a couple of two leafers?"

"As I said before . . ." Elizabeth grinned. A field mouse burst from a corner of the wall and darted off, disappearing in the brilliant green of the grass. For about the fiftieth time today Elizabeth thought about the beauty of Bannerman's Estate. She looked down at the clover. "I think you should have half of it. Just—just in case."

"Oh, you don't have to do that!" Todd protested, but Elizabeth pulled gently. The clover came apart at the seam, with two leaves on each side.

"Here you go," she said. Her throat felt dry as she handed one half of the clover to Todd.

Slowly Todd slid his hand into Elizabeth's and took the clover. Their fingertips touched. And stayed touching for a fraction of a second.

"Thanks, Elizabeth," Todd said. Carefully he placed his half of the clover inside his shirt pocket.

Elizabeth smiled. Somewhere birds were singing. But whether they were in real life or only in her head, she wasn't sure.

"Anytime," she said.

Jessica walked along a trail, practically in tears. Not only had she lost Aaron just when she thought she'd maybe gotten him back, but now she looked worse than ever.

Her fingers and knees were covered with mud from when she'd rolled into the bushes. There were angry red scratches up and down her arms. Not to mention the sores on her face, the dirt on her wrists, and the poison ivy on her ankles. Her hair was crawling with insects. A caterpillar had just fallen out of her shirt, and she had bug bites from head to toe.

Plus she was hopelessly lost. The trails all

crossed and recrossed, most of them didn't seem to be marked, some of them stopped right in the middle of nothing, and she'd had to cross through a swamp, which left her in stinking greenish black water up to her knees.

She slapped halfheartedly at another mosquito, which was trying to suck out the little blood she had left, and peered up ahead, where the trail curved. Jessica thought she could hear voices. She quickened her pace. Maybe she was almost there. Wherever "there" was.

"Cowabunga!" someone shouted.

The lake. Jessica rounded the bend and stopped short. Ahead of her stretched the cool crystal waters of the camp's lake. It looked beautiful, and Jessica considered just plunging in with all her clothes on. She could see herself running across the sandy beach and diving into the water. No possible way could she come out worse than she went in. It was awfully tempting.

Slowly Jessica took a step forward. Too bad there were people around.

"Hey, Asher, check this one out!" another voice yelled.

Jessica froze. Just to the left of her stood Dennis Asher, a towel wrapped loosely around his neck.

Cute, she thought, putting her hands on her hips and staring at him. He couldn't see her, but she could definitely see him. *Definitely cute.* Funny how she hadn't much noticed Dennis Asher before.

Maybe it was because she'd had a sort-of boyfriend up until, like, ten minutes ago.

Jessica remembered Aaron's telling her that Dennis was the guy that Aaron blamed for having a hard night last night. She felt her lips curve into a smile. If Dennis had been giving Aaron a hard time, then he obviously was a good guy.

"Ah, I can do that too," Dennis shouted to someone on the float twenty yards out into the lake. Dropping his towel on the beach, he swam expertly out to the float himself. Jessica watched as he clambered onto the platform and executed a perfect swan dive into the clear blue water.

Jessica's heart raced. Drop-dead gorgeous—and talented. She stepped forward toward Dennis, putting her foot carefully over a mud puddle. Then she stopped. A mud puddle. She'd suddenly remembered how she looked. Her messed-up hair, her scratched face, the mosquito bites, the caked-in mud.

She wasn't exactly in boy-getting mode.

Why, oh why, couldn't he have noticed me before this? When I was pretty?

Turning slowly, Jessica walked back down the trail, cursing her rotten luck. And the person who had brought her such rotten luck. The King of Mean. Aaron Dallas.

"Trust him to ruin my life," she mumbled miserably as she walked on.

Seven

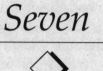

"There's a hawk overhead; I can see it in the sky," Elizabeth read slowly to herself. "With the hawk overhead, I could learn to soar and fly."

Yes. She nodded. That would do just fine.

Not that she'd actually seen a hawk here at camp. Not *yet*.

Elizabeth was sitting on a grassy stretch of ground near the infirmary. She'd signed up for a poetry workshop with Mr. Bowman, her favorite teacher, and she was loving every minute of it. The assignment had been to write about camp in some way, and Elizabeth's only problem had been to narrow down the possibilities.

She wondered what kind of a poem the Unicorns would write. It would probably go, "Camp is stupid, camp is dumb; gee, I wish we'd never come." Or, "Camp is no fun at all; get me out of here and to a mall." She smiled. If she lived to be a thousand, she would never understand Jessica and her friends.

"With the hawk overhead, I could go explore a cloud," she wrote. "Like the hawk overhead, I would fly—"

She frowned. *Loud* didn't seem quite right. "Groud? Noud? Boud?" she muttered. *No. Crowd, soud, plowed . . .*

Proud. She grinned. *Of course.* "Like the hawk overhead," she repeated, erasing the last couple of words, "I'd fly straight and true and proud."

"I wish we'd never come," Ellen said, lying on her sleeping bag later that afternoon in the Unicorns' tent. "I thought this was going to be a really cool trip, but so far it hasn't been. The bathrooms are disgusting, and my hair is ruined, and I think they pitched this stupid tent on quicksand or something. I can feel it getting lower and lower, like, every minute."

Jessica was too miserable to say anything. They'd just gotten back from Mrs. Arnette's class, which had been ten times more boring than her wildest dreams. And after everything else that had happened today . . .

"We're here because camp was required, doofus," Kimberly snapped. "Because they'd call the truant officer and have us put in jail if we stayed home."

"I don't care." Ellen clutched her head and

moaned. "The truant officer would be better than *this*. So would jail. In jail you don't have to spend all your time outdoors. They give you a nice cell with a floor and a ceiling and even walls."

"It's not that bad," Mandy said softly. "But I *am* a little worried about my hair. I don't think all these leaves and twigs are going to come out easily."

"You think leaves are the worst of your problems?" Janet asked, raising an eyebrow. "Well, you're so wrong, it isn't even funny. I could feel, like, spiders laying eggs in my hair all night long. Spiders and mosquitoes and caterpillars too. The kind that even six bottles of industrial-strength shampoo won't get rid of."

"Janet's right," Lila said with feeling. "I've never seen so many bugs in my entire life. And every time I turn around, my face gets windburn."

"Windburn?" Janet laughed hollowly. "And you think *that's* serious. You should have seen how close *I* came to sunstroke. They almost sent me to the infirmary." She paused. "Which wouldn't have been so bad, come to think of it."

"Outdoor living," Kimberly said, her eyes flashing, "is disgusting."

"Even *school* would be better than this." Ellen's voice was muffled by the sleeping bag. "That class with the Hairnet was, like, the *worst*."

Usually Jessica laughed when someone called Mrs. Arnette the Hairnet. But today she was too unhappy to even smile.

Mandy rolled her eyes. "I think the only person who liked it was Randy Mason."

"You mean, the only person who stayed *awake* was Randy Mason." Kimberly yawned. "*I* certainly didn't. *I* fell asleep after ten minutes."

"You lasted ten minutes?" Lila made a face. "*I* fell asleep after five minutes."

"Oh, you did not either." Kimberly snorted.

"Not that it matters," Janet informed them haughtily, "but *I* fell asleep after only *two* minutes. Maybe even *one*." She glared around the cramped tent as if daring any of the other girls to deny it.

Jessica sighed and rolled over, though just stretching her leg was pure torture. Sometimes the other Unicorns could be so irritating. As if *their* problems could possibly compare to *hers*. Sure, most of them were dirty, especially Janet, and most of them were scratched, especially Mandy, and lots of them had messy hair, especially Lila, but none of them had as many mosquito bites, except Kimberly, or as much poison ivy, except Ellen. And maybe Lila and Janet.

And none of them had lost a boyfriend already that morning. The thought of Aaron made Jessica feel lonely and miserable. And the thought of Dennis Asher made her feel even worse. He was *so* gorgeous, and she was *so* disgusting. . . .

"Like we'd be interested in the history of this stupid place," Kimberly said with a sniff. "Did you guys catch that line about the invention of that dumb idiotic birdcall tape recorder?" She hugged her knees. "Like we *care.*"

"Yeah, that part was totally bogus," Lila said disdainfully.

"Birdcalls," Janet agreed. "Like people actually spend their lives listening to birdcalls. And when she played those examples for us!" She made gagging noises.

"Randy Mason liked it," Mandy said doubtfully. "He knew lots of the birds too."

"Yeah, well, he *would,*" Kimberly said. "And what was it Mrs. Arnette said? 'My, Randy, the gentleman who invented this machine would be proud of you!'" she quoted in a squeaky voice. "Good thing that was almost at the end. I practically barfed."

"Me too," Lila said.

"I *did* barf," Janet said. "A little bit. I would have barfed even more if they'd served us a decent lunch instead of that vomitrocious stew."

Jessica frowned. *But if that part had come at the end of the lecture, then how—?* "I thought you guys were asleep," she ventured.

"Yeah, Lila," Janet said, sitting up straight and scratching a mosquito bite. "I thought you were asleep."

"Um—" Lila looked down at the ground and blushed.

Kimberly shrugged. "We *were* asleep. At least, I was. But that part was so bad, I just *had* to wake up."

"Speaking of vomitrocious," Ellen said wearily, "what's for dinner?"

"I hope it's pizza," Mandy murmured.

"Yeah, maybe they could order out." Kimberly held an imaginary phone to her ear. "Three thousand slices of pepperoni pizza to go, please."

"Don't forget sausage." Ellen licked her lips.

"And Camembert," Lila put in.

And pineapple, Jessica thought. *But it'll probably be Chicken à la Gross or Fruit Salad with Worms instead.* Not only did she look awful. Not only was she a food supply for bugs. Not only was she dirty and smelly and totally disgusting *and* without a boyfriend, but she was also going to starve to death.

Some great time to finally notice Dennis Asher.

"When we get home, we're ordering a pizza with all the toppings in the world," Kimberly promised. "And extra everything. Even if there's only, like, six dollars in the club treasury."

Jessica tried to smile, but it hurt too much. Shutting her eyes, she felt the rough edge of her sleeping bag against her cheek. Dennis Asher's face floated dreamily in her mind. Dennis and Jessica. Jessica and Dennis.

Jessicandennis.

She sighed. There was no chance of bagging him. Not this week anyway.

"Oh, my monster, oh, my monster, oh, my monster Frankenstein!" Elizabeth sang along with most of the other middle-school kids that evening.

She caught Todd's eye and winked. They were sharing a log around a huge campfire that sparked and glowed in the darkness. In the distance Elizabeth could hear crickets chirping and the gentle rustling of leaves on the trees overhead.

The perfect night, she thought happily. Sharing a log and roasted marshmallows around a campfire with your sort-of boyfriend. After a day of romantic walks and writing poetry in the middle of nature. What could be better?

"You were built to last forever, oh, my monster Frankenstein!" the kids sang.

Elizabeth smiled and shifted her weight so her knee was almost brushing up against Todd's.

Nothing could be better, she thought happily. That was what!

"How about 'Tom the Toad'?" Amy Sutton suggested.

"Oh, *please*," Janet said, rolling her eyes.

Jessica sighed. First "Old MacDonald" on the bus yesterday. And now "Tom the Toad." *Great.* "How about Johnny Buck?" she suggested. Even something by Elvis or the Beatles or some of those other ancient guys would be better than stupid juvenile songs like these.

"Hey, yeah!" Kimberly turned to her. But it was too late. All around the campfire kids were starting to sing.

Jessica considered covering her ears. It was too

bad that ears didn't just shut like eyes. "Oh, Tom the Toad, oh, Tom the Toad," the kids sang, "why did you jump out on the road?" Jessica groaned.

Elizabeth seemed to be singing loudest of all. Jessica could see her sister clearly, sitting with Todd on the other side of the campfire. The bright orange flames crackled and hissed. Her sister still looked gorgeous, she thought hollowly. It wasn't fair.

"You did not see the car ahead!" the kids sang boisterously, but Jessica just stared bleakly across at Elizabeth. It wasn't even close to being fair.

"And now you're wearing tire tread!" There was a jealous ache in the pit of Jessica's stomach. Here was Elizabeth, sharing marshmallows with her boyfriend, while Jessica was sharing marshmallows with mosquitoes.

"Oh, Tom the Toad, oh, Tom the Toad," the kids chorused, "why did you jump out on the road?"

That's me, Tom the Toad, Jessica thought, swallowing hard. The acrid smell of campfire smoke filled her lungs, and she coughed. *My whole day's been like Tom the Toad's. Aaron ran over me just like the car that squooshed Tom. And now I'm all alone and—*

"You just kept going hop, hop, hop," Elizabeth, Todd, and the rest sang out. "But that car wouldn't stop, stop, stop."

Pangs of envy overtook Jessica. She couldn't even make a play for a real hot guy like Dennis Asher because she looked so awful. While Elizabeth sat with a wimp like Todd, and she had not one single solitary hair out of place. It was *not fair*.

"Hey, don't you guys know the last verse to that song?" Jessica's heart skipped a beat. The voice belonged to Dennis.

"You mean there's more?" Randy Mason furrowed his brow.

Lila cast an irritated glance at Jessica. "There *would* be," she muttered.

Dennis nodded. Jessica could just make out his face, about thirty people down the circle from her. "Sure," he said confidently. "It goes like this."

"Oh, great, he's going to sing some more," Janet hissed. "Pardon me while I die."

"'Don't play in roads,' said his old mom," Dennis warbled. Despite herself Jessica leaned forward, anxious to hear his voice. He sang well, she realized. Though he would do a better job with Johnny Buck. "And now she mourns for her dear Tom!"

"Oh, Tom the Toad, oh, Tom the Toad!" the other kids sang back. "Why did you jump out on the road?"

Dennis sat back down as the group applauded. But Jessica just stared at the ground.

It was absolutely, positively, totally, one hundred percent not fair.

"Attention!"

Winston Egbert flung his arms into the air. "Winston the Magnificent will now tell you the untold history of the Bannerman Estate," he announced in a ghostly voice.

Aaron suppressed a snicker. "Is it going to be more interesting than the stuff we learned about in class today?" he yelled.

"Can you doubt it?" Even in the semidarkness Aaron could see that Winston looked shocked. "Of course! I, Winston the Magnificent, teller of tales that are truer than true, will tell you the true and telling tale of the two twins and the—and the—um—" He scratched his head. "And the guy they wanted to marry," he continued in a more normal voice.

Aaron snorted. *Marry. Good grief.* No self-respecting guy would ever *want* to get married. Having a sort-of girlfriend was one thing, but you didn't want to get too serious. Of course, girls didn't always understand the way guys did things. Like Jessica this morning. It wasn't like he'd *meant* to hurt her feelings or anything; it was just that she was right there and it seemed like it would be so easy to play a great trick on her. But she was a girl and his sort-of girlfriend, and so she'd gone and taken it personally.

Aaron made a face and scuffed the heel of his tennis shoe into the dirt. He could see Jessica sitting with some of her friends off to the side, looking miserable. *Poor kid.* He felt almost a little sorry for her.

But it wouldn't make sense to try to talk to her. She'd probably demand an apology. And how could a guy apologize when he hadn't even done anything wrong? It was just a joke. Any guy would have teased her. About bears and all. He sighed. *Women.*

"My story is positively guaranteed genuine or your money back," Winston explained, gesturing expansively to his audience. In the firelight Aaron thought Winston looked even weirder than usual. "And it happened here in *this exact camp,* and even right here on *this very spot.*" He dropped his voice to a stage whisper.

Aaron smirked. *Yeah, right,* he thought, wondering if the story would be about bears. Idly he attached a marshmallow to the end of his stick and thrust it into the fire. *Yeah. Bears.* He grinned. Now *that* would be interesting.

"This happened about a hundred and fifty years ago," Winston said, keeping his voice low. "Right here, where I am standing, there was a small house, and in this house there lived twin girls."

"How old were the girls?" Amy Sutton called out.

"Eighteen," Winston said without missing a beat. "I mean, eighteen each. Thirty-six altogether."

Aaron stroked the back of his neck. He'd gotten a little sun today. So the girls were older than the Wakefield twins. He glanced at Jessica again, wondering if maybe he ought to say something to her. Maybe it wouldn't have to be, like, a real apology. Maybe he could just sort of—

"And they wanted to get married," Winston went on. "The only problem was, they loved the same man."

He paused. It was quiet around the campfire. Aaron felt a sudden chill in the air. His hand groped for the flashlight he'd brought with him. There was something just a little—well, a little unsettling about the way Winston had spoken those last words. "What was his name? Johnny Buck?" he called out, hoping to break the tension.

"The man's name," Winston intoned, "is lost in the sands of time. But I can assure you that he was not the immortal Buckster."

A few people laughed. Aaron hauled the marshmallow out of the fire. *Great. Burned.*

"They loved the same man," Winston went on, his voice eerie in the night, "and each one tried to impress him and get him to marry her. But he would always tell them that he couldn't choose. 'I can barely tell you two apart!' he'd say."

Ha, Aaron thought contemptuously. He'd always been able to tell the Wakefield twins apart. Always. Just by instinct. He began to lose interest in the story.

"And so he insisted that the girls choose," Winston went on. "'The day the two of you tell me which one I shall marry, then the next day shall be our wedding day,' he said."

Wimp, Aaron thought. Yawning, he gazed off into the bushes. Yeah, that had been Jessica he'd played that joke on, for sure. No question.

And it had been a pretty good joke at that.

In fact . . .

Aaron began to grin to himself, remembering the panic he'd caused at the boys' camp.

Remembering the look on Jessica's face when she'd run from the bear that didn't even exist.

He stared off into the dark ring of forest that surrounded the campfire.

Twice wasn't enough for a really rad practical joke like the bear one.

His hand tightened on the flashlight. Maybe, just maybe, it was time to do it again.

Eight

"And so," Winston was saying in a mysterious voice, "late one night, when the full moon was low on the horizon, the twins made a deal."

Despite herself Jessica felt a tingle of fear. She'd expected that Winston would make a big joke out of the story. Maybe he would in the end, but just now he was telling the story like a master fisherman, keeping them all dangling in suspense like the worm at the end of his line.

She wondered if the story was really true.

Winston paused for effect. "They took a silver dollar that their mother had left them," he said, "a coin that their mother had given them the night before she died, and they flipped it."

"They what?" Kimberly asked.

"They flipped it," Winston repeated, demonstrating

with his thumb. "And one of the girls called it in the air: 'Heads!'" he barked suddenly, catching an imaginary coin in his outstretched palm. "And the other girl opened her fingers, slowly, one by one, to reveal—"

With painful slowness Winston unraveled one finger at a time.

"It was tails," he said ominously.

Jessica shook her head. *What a dumb way to choose a husband.*

"Is this a ghost story?" Lila demanded.

"A ghost story?" Winston asked thoughtfully. Silhouetted against the fire, he stretched his arms out slowly. "Listen."

Jessica frowned. There was something . . . strange about Winston's story. Something that had a certain meaning for her, if she only knew where to look. . . .

"Together the twins went to the young man's house," Winston said softly. "They told him that he now had a wife, and the winning sister stepped forward. 'Is this true?' the man asked the other sister. Her eyes were sad, but she said yes. And they planned the wedding for the next day."

Jessica took a quick look around the circle. There was Elizabeth, next to Todd. Were they still holding hands? She thought they were. Randy Mason, a thoughtful expression on his face. Aaron Dallas, looking at the ground, fiddling with something she couldn't quite see.

"So what's the punch line, Egbert?" Bruce Patman broke in.

"Punch line?" Winston asked. "What makes you think there's a punch line? That night," he continued, dropping his voice to a half whisper, "the sister who lost stayed awake till her twin was asleep. Then she crept out of bed and into the kitchen."

Despite herself Jessica held her breath, suspecting she knew what would happen next. She strained to figure out how the story could be important to her. Something about twins, that was obvious. And about husbands? But she was only twelve, a *long* way from having a husband. . . .

"She chose the longest, straightest, sharpest knife she could." Winston bit off each word. "And she went into the bedroom and held the knife over her sister's heart, and then, with a sudden motion—" Winston leaped forward and brought his arm crashing down. Ellen screamed.

"Did she die?" Lila asked fearfully.

"She died," Winston said in a mournful voice that seemed to echo and reecho off the nearby pines. "She died instantly. And her sister hid the body in the storage shed. She even changed the sheets so there would be no bloodstains."

Jessica shuddered. Never in her wildest dreams had she seriously considered killing her sister, though she had been sorely tempted more than once. *That woman must have been sick,* she thought.

"Bright and early the next morning the killer

went to the man's house," Winston said. "'I've come for our wedding,' she said to him, and he never suspected a thing. So they got hitched, and when the man asked where the other sister was, the killer said, 'Oh, she isn't feeling good,' which was sort of true, and they moved into the twins' house that night."

Into the twins' house. There was an uneasy feeling in Jessica's stomach.

"And everything was fine for a few days," Winston said, "until—"

"Until the body started to stink," Bruce suggested.

Winston shook his head. "Until the ghost started to get into the act." He paused. "Its first appearance was late at night, by a hollow oak tree. It stared at the young husband and held up a silver dollar, but it said nothing at all. The husband came home and told his wife about it, and she said—"

"A bear!" Another, louder voice rang out over Winston's.

A bear? Jessica didn't stop to figure out who was speaking.

She just stood up and started to run.

"Get out of here, quick!" Aaron was shouting. "A bear, a big one!"

A bear? Elizabeth swung around, tightening her grip on Todd's hand. Her heart lurched. Aaron clicked a flashlight off and on and stared into the forest, wide-eyed with fear. "A bear! A real one! I'm not kidding! Better run!"

Instinctively Elizabeth shrank back. Her eyes searched for escape routes.

"Run!" Lila shouted from across the campfire. Behind her Elizabeth could just make out the shape of her sister disappearing into the night.

"Help!" Ellen screamed. She waved her arms frantically, almost as if she were trying to fly. "Helphelphelp!"

"Oh, man," Amy said uncertainly. She bit her lip and stared at Elizabeth. "But which way should we go?"

"Get up, quick!" Todd hissed in Elizabeth's ear.

Aaron swung the flashlight so its beam pointed off into the woods. "Shift into overdrive!" he cried. "It's . . . it's . . . it's coming this way! Hurry!"

Todd steered Elizabeth toward the path that led back to the campsites. "Stay calm," he whispered urgently. "Stay calm—stay—" He paused. "Wait a minute."

"What is it?" Elizabeth's tongue felt all furry. She could barely get the words out. A real bear was much more frightening than some old ghost story that probably wasn't even true. Her eyes strained to make out the onrushing bear. "What's the problem?"

"That's Dallas," Todd said softly. "And last night he—well, never mind." He took a step forward. "Hey, Aaron!" he shouted over the hubbub of the crowd. "This the same bear you saw last night or what?"

Aaron aimed his flashlight steadily at the

forest's edge. "Right there!" he called. "It's definitely a bear! Look at the claws, at the teeth!"

Todd looked disgusted. "Dallas!" he barked.
"That's a tree trunk, and you know it!"

"A tree trunk?" Aaron said in a totally uncon-
vincing voice. "Are you positive, Wilkins?" He took
a couple of steps closer to the "bear." "Wow!" he
said after a moment. "Well, what do you know?"

A tree trunk? Slowly Elizabeth's heart returned to
normal. Now that she knew there was no bear, she
couldn't believe she'd ever thought there might
have been one. She took a deep breath. Yes, it was
definitely a tree trunk. The steady beam of the flashlight proved it. She shook her head, feeling embarrassed for ever having believed Aaron to begin with.

"Oh, come *on*." Todd turned away and rolled his
eyes. "False alarm, guys," he announced at the top
of his lungs. "Just Dallas here, needing to have his
eyes checked."

"Aw, I knew it all along," Bruce boasted as he
dropped down from the branch he'd clambered up.
"Dumb joke, Dallas."

"You mean that was only a joke?" Elizabeth recognized Lila's voice, angry and fearful at the same time.
"So I've gone and broken three nails for nothing?"

"Beware, the dangerous tree trunk," Todd said,
catching Elizabeth's eye.

Elizabeth couldn't help laughing. "Eyes like fire
and claws like, um—"

"Razor blades," Todd finished for her. "Hey,

Winston, better add this story to your list. 'The Night Aaron Dallas Got Spooked by a Tree Trunk.'" He rested his elbow on Elizabeth's shoulder and glared at Aaron. "It was a dark and stormy night, and Aaron Dallas was being a total doofus—I mean, Aaron Doofus was being a total Dallas—"

"Like he says," Elizabeth added, jerking her thumb at Todd.

"I thought he was making it up," Randy said. "A bear wouldn't attack a whole group of people like this. It's not what bears do."

Amy shook her head and glared at Aaron as she resumed her seat on the log. "Very funny, Aaron," she told him.

Aaron grinned. "Well, it looked like a bear anyway," he said with satisfaction. "And you guys all looked so incredibly stupid running away! Ha, ha, ha!"

"Real mature, Dallas," Todd said bitterly. He led Elizabeth back to their seat. "Next time why don't you go pick on somebody with a brain your size, huh?"

"Because," Aaron said, narrowing his eyes, "no one else in this entire school has a brain as big as mine!"

It was well past ten o'clock, and Jessica was exhausted. But she hadn't been able to fall asleep.

She'd listened to chirping crickets until she thought she'd go insane. She'd crawled in and out of her sleeping bag, trying to get to a comfortable temperature, until half of her was sweating and the other half was like ice. And she could have drawn a detailed map of all the sticks, stones, and little tiny hills under her spot in the tent. *I'm just like the princess in that story about the princess and the pea*, she told herself drowsily. The one who could feel the pea through twenty mattresses. For a fleeting moment she wondered if maybe she did have royal blood.

But sticks and stones weren't what was keeping her awake.

Jessica sighed and unzipped her sleeping bag a little further. No. Something was still bothering her about Winston's story. It had been a pretty dumb story when you came right down to it, she told herself. Still . . .

"So the twins wanted to marry the same guy," she whispered, her words floating in the air. Well, that didn't fit her situation. Elizabeth had Todd, right? She was welcome to him. Todd was perfectly nice, but he was one of the most boring kids in the sixth grade, even if Elizabeth had always refused to believe it when Jessica was giving her some sisterly advice.

So that wasn't it. What else? Jessica shifted uncomfortably inside her sleeping bag. Now she was too cold. Carefully she zipped the bag up just a couple of inches, wishing she had a real bed with real blankets. *It's like there's an important moral here somewhere*, she told herself, straining to think. *An important moral.*

Not about murder. Though after what Aaron had pulled tonight—again!—she didn't think any jury would ever put her in jail if she did decide to strangle her ex-sort-of-boyfriend. She reflected again on possible morals of the story. *And not about keeping sharp knives out of your kitchen.* Though that wasn't such a bad idea either. No. Something else. Something about . . . about being a twin.

Jessica held her breath. It was on the tip of her tongue. . . .

In the wilderness something made a noise. *Probably a wildcat,* Jessica thought with a shudder, wondering if a wildcat could tell the difference between her and her sister if it decided to eat just one of them—

And then suddenly she had her answer.

Jessica sat up straight in the darkness. "That's it!" she whispered excitedly.

The twins had decided they were too old this year for their annual April Fools' switch. But maybe they weren't after all. At least maybe *she* wasn't. Maybe she'd pull a switch, just like the two girls did in Winston's story.

She had a plan—a plan for catching Dennis Asher. A plan that involved Elizabeth. But the beauty of it was, Elizabeth didn't even need to know about it. Just like in Winston's story, again. The twin who had no idea there'd be a switcheroo. Only, of course, Jessica wouldn't have to *kill* Elizabeth.

Slowly, contentedly Jessica settled back down, ignoring the snake hole under her hip. She clasped her hands behind her neck and stared happily at the ceiling of the tent.

Things were truly looking up.

Nine

◇

Lila opened one eye. Somewhere nearby Charlie Cashman was playing his trumpet. If *playing* was the right word.

She sighed and burrowed deeper into her sleeping bag. She wished Charlie would go away. She wished camp would go away. Here it was, only Tuesday, and she was already sick of it. Totally sick of it.

"Will somebody tell that stupid kid to shut up?" Janet moaned.

"Yeah," Kimberly added. "Can he please get a life and put that cow back where he found it?"

Laughing would have taken too much energy. Lila shut her eyes. Between the spiders, the mosquitoes, the mud, the roots, the campfire smoke, the poison ivy, and the lack of any civilized beauty salon, Lila was pretty sure her looks were ruined for life. What was the point of getting up when you looked the way she did?

"Well, I'm going back to sleep," Janet announced.

Lila nodded sleepily. That was what she was going to do too. Outside the tent she could hear soft voices and scuffling feet. *Kids getting up,* she told herself, and then rephrased it. *Nutty* kids getting up. Who in their right mind would actually *want* to get up at three A.M. or whatever stupid time it was?

"We'll miss breakfast again," Mandy said in a worried tone.

"Breakfast, breakfast," Kimberly muttered. "So who cares about breakfast?"

Lila did care about breakfast, but not enough to actually crawl out of her warm sleeping bag. "Come on, guys," she said, stifling a yawn. "You're making too much noise. Some of us are trying to sleep."

"Yeah, well, if you wouldn't *talk* so much, Lila," Kimberly began.

"Quiet, everybody," Janet commanded. "As club president I insist that everybody go back to sleep."

"And what if we get in trouble?" Mandy asked.

"We won't," Janet assured her. "And if we do, it's like that movie about those three guys in France. You know, all for one and one for all?"

Lila nodded and yawned. She'd seen that movie, all about the three friends who were, like, soldiers, and who named their club after a candy bar for some strange reason. "Yeah," she said slowly. "We'll help each other out."

"You mean, like, we won't rat on each other?" Ellen asked.

"Well, that too," Janet said importantly. "But we'll lie for each other also because that's what club members do. If anybody asks, we'll just say we were there."

"Where?" Ellen asked.

"Wherever everybody else was!" Lila said impatiently. *Gee, Ellen can sure be dense sometimes.* "Like if they say, 'Where was Ellen during assembly,' I'll say I saw you at assembly, and Kimberly will say *she* saw you at assembly—"

"And I'll say *I* saw you at assembly," Janet interrupted. "Do we all agree? And then we need to get back to sleep."

"I agree," Lila said sleepily.

"Me too," Kimberly said.

"We need to do this by roll call," Janet said. "All in favor, say aye. Lila?"

Lila sighed. "I just said it," she pointed out, wishing everybody would shut up and leave her alone.

Janet snorted. "Well, say it again!"

"Aye," Lila said quickly. She turned onto her back and tried to stay perfectly still.

"Ellen?"

"Oh, *aye*," Ellen said with feeling. "Aye and double aye."

"Jessica?"

There was silence.

"Jessica?" Janet repeated.

No one spoke. Lila slowly opened one eye and turned her head toward Jessica's sleeping bag.

"Jes-si-ca!" Janet barked.

Lila blinked and rubbed her eyes. *Weird*, she thought uneasily.

Jessica's sleeping bag was empty.

Jessica didn't think she'd ever gotten up so early in her life. She'd actually stolen out of the tent a few minutes before Charlie Cashman had even started blowing his so-called trumpet, just in case any of her friends gave her a hard time. Much as she would have liked to wait for them and sleep some more, she couldn't. Not if she wanted to put her plan into action.

Now she was standing in the early morning shadows near the bulletin board, which listed the day's activities, waiting for a certain person to come and sign up.

Most of the kids were ignoring her, which was just as well. It was best to stay as anonymous as she could. Besides which, getting up early in the morning always made her bleary-eyed. And there was still no way she was showering in rotten-egg water, so she was sure she was looking even worse than last night. If that was possible.

Jessica yawned and thrust her hands into her pockets to keep them warm. It was cooler than she'd expected. For about the fifth time she scanned the list of afternoon activities and classes. *Orienteering (whatever that was) . . . canoeing lessons . . . poetry work-shop . . . the history of Bannerman's Estate . . . nature study . . . archaeological dig . . . volleyball instruction . . .*

Most of the lists were getting pretty long. Except for the Hairnet's history class, which was practically empty. Jessica hoped Dennis would show up soon so he wouldn't have to register for that one. *Canoeing wouldn't be bad,* she thought. *Or volleyball.*

She sneaked anxious looks left and right. Where was Dennis?

A group of eighth-graders approached the bulletin board and signed their names boldly under "volleyball." *So much for that idea,* Jessica told herself. The volleyball list was now full.

Jessica shifted her weight uneasily from one foot to the other. She hadn't seen any of the other Unicorns yet this morning. They were probably still asleep. She hoped Dennis wasn't like her friends. But what if he was? What if he was the kind of guy who slept, like, practically all the time?

Then she would have gotten up early for nothing, that's what.

As if camp wasn't bad enough already without having to get up at two o'clock in the morning or whatever stupid time it had been. Here it was, not even eight yet, and already it felt as though she'd been awake for—

Jessica froze. A familiar face was approaching the bulletin board.

Quickly Jessica moved halfway behind an old

spruce tree. Dennis was alone, she was pleased to see, and he was jauntily whistling a Johnny Buck tune. Grabbing the marker that hung in front of the bulletin board, he scanned the list carefully, shaking his head from time to time.

Jessica watched, hoping like crazy that he wouldn't sign up for the Hairnet.

Dennis ran his hand through his hair. "Too bad about the volleyball," he announced to no one in particular.

Jessica held her breath. *Not history*, she urged him via ESP. *Not history . . . not history . . .*

Dennis uncapped the marker and scrawled his name on the canoeing sheet. "Let's hit the boats!" he said, punching his fist into the air. Then he let the marker drop and dashed off.

Canoeing. That would be just fine. Heaving a sigh of relief, Jessica walked boldly out from behind the tree.

"Canoeing for me too," she murmured to herself, writing quickly and reattaching the marker to its string.

She stepped back to admire her handiwork.

Number fifteen on the canoeing list was Dennis Asher.

And number sixteen was . . . Elizabeth Wakefield.

"Elizabeth! What are you doing here?"

Elizabeth looked questioningly at her friend Maria Slater. It was later that day, and she was sorting balls of string for the macramé class she and Todd had signed up for. "What do you mean?" she asked. "This is macramé, isn't it? I signed up for this class."

"You did?" Maria frowned.

Elizabeth thought back just to be sure. She and Todd had signed up practically first thing this morning, before almost anybody else, to make sure they'd get the same project. "What's the problem?" she asked. The heading on the list had definitely said "Macramé," she was positive.

"Oh—nothing." Maria shook her head. "I could have sworn I saw your name at the bottom of the canoeing sheet is all. Like the last name on the list." She shrugged. "I was thinking about signing up for that one, but it was full when I got there."

Elizabeth frowned. *On the canoeing sheet?* She and Todd hadn't considered signing up for that one. "I . . . I don't think so," she said, scratching her head. She couldn't imagine how her name could have gotten onto the canoeing list.

Maria nodded. "I wondered, actually, because it didn't look exactly like your writing. Not as neat, you know? And the *E* looked funny." She shrugged. "Well, it doesn't matter. And I'm glad we're in the same workshop."

"Me too," Elizabeth said. She smiled at Maria and went back to the string. Funny how her name had turned up on the wrong list.

But there had to be a reasonable explanation.

There always was.

* * *

Jessica stood on the dock, which overlooked the lake, waiting for the canoeing class to start. None of her friends were in it. Usually that would have been a real bummer, but this wasn't usually. Today, in fact, Jessica was grateful that she didn't know the other kids very well.

Nearby sat Dennis Asher, alone on the dock, whistling and trailing his feet in the water. He hadn't noticed her yet.

Jessica's heart hammered. She took a deep breath. It was now or never.

"Hi," she said shyly, stooping down to Dennis's level. "You're Dennis, right?"

Dennis looked up. For a fraction of a second his lip curled, and Jessica thought he was going to say something obnoxious about the way she looked. But he didn't. "That's right," he agreed. "Do I know you?"

Jessica shrugged. "Not really," she told him. *Which was the understatement of the century.* "But I know *you*. I'm—um—" She swallowed hard. "Elizabeth. Wakefield, that is." There. She'd done it.

Dennis nodded solemnly. "Nice to meet you."

"Nice to meet *you*," Jessica said. "Listen, I, um, wanted to talk to you about something."

Dennis gazed out across the lake and splashed the water with his bare heel. "Sure," he said. "What is it?"

Jessica steeled her nerves. "It's about my, um, sister."

Dennis raised his eyebrows and swiveled to face Jessica. "You have a sister? Is she here at camp?"

Jessica nodded. That much was true anyway. "Her name's Jessica," she said brightly. "She looks just like me, only she's, you know, cleaner?"

Dennis gave an easy laugh. "No offense or anything, but that wouldn't be too hard," he said. His eye ran down Jessica from head to foot.

"Tell me about it!" Jessica tried to hide her irritation. *Curses on the mosquitoes,* she told herself angrily. *Curses on the mud and the swamp and the poison ivy. And curses on the stupid rotten-egg water.* She plunged ahead before she could turn pink underneath all that grime. "And—well—there's, like, no easy way to tell you this, I guess, but—" She hesitated, wondering exactly how to put it into words. "I mean—Jessica, my sister—she, um—"

"She has a crush on me," Dennis guessed.

Jessica leaned back in surprise, almost losing her balance in the process. "How . . . how did you know?"

Dennis smiled. "Lots of girls had crushes on me. At my old school. So this sister of yours, she looks like you except cleaner?" He wrinkled his nose.

Jessica's hand flew up to her cheek. "Yeah, cleaner," she agreed. "And, um, a tiny bit prettier. I mean, we're identical twins, but we don't look *exactly* alike," she lied. "Everybody always says Jessica is prettier than I am." *And if they don't, they should.*

Dennis nodded slowly. "Uh-huh," he said. "So, um, how am I going to get to know this sister of yours?"

He's buying it! Jessica could feel her heart

pumping faster. "Well, that's just it," she said. "She's really shy. Too shy to tell you herself."

"So she sent you to tell me, is that it?" Dennis reached down and ran his fingers lightly along the surface of the water.

"Well—sort of. I mean, yeah." Jessica was having a hard time keeping straight just who was who here. "Now, like, if you come on real strong this week, she'll probably get scared." It wouldn't do to have Dennis get *too* close to Elizabeth, she realized. Her little twin switch wouldn't last too long if Elizabeth and Dennis actually had conversations that lasted more than about three seconds. "But just kind of *notice* her this week," Jessica went on boldly. "Let her know that you're, like, looking at her and you think she's really pretty and all that. Smile at her. That kind of stuff." She took a deep breath. "And maybe next week at school she'll start smiling at you."

After I get a real shower, that is, she told herself. *And have my hair done. And do something about these mosquito bites and broken nails and zits all over my cheeks that I got from being allergic to nature.* She smiled, thinking about it. Yup. Dennis would stare at Elizabeth all week long and get really interested. And then Jessica would look like herself again next week, and she'd saunter down the hallway, and flash him a little smile, and maybe say, "Hi, Dennis!" and—

And she could take it from there.

Oh, yes, she could *definitely* take it from there.

"So I should notice her," Dennis said as if trying to

puzzle it all out. "But I shouldn't, like, get too close."

Relief washed over Jessica. *This could actually work,* she told herself. "Exactly right," she said.

"OK," Dennis said, grinning at Jessica. "Thanks for the tip, Elizabeth. If she's really cleaner *and* prettier than you, then maybe she'll even be worth it." He kicked up a shower of water just as the teacher in charge of the canoes blew a whistle.

Cleaner *and* prettier? Jessica didn't much like the sound of that. She was about to snarl at Dennis, but then she remembered she was supposed to be being Elizabeth and that it was Jessica who was supposed to be prettier, which meant her very own self even if it was really Elizabeth. . . . She sighed. The next few days had the potential to be very confusing.

"There's only one other thing," she told him as they made their way toward the end of the dock. "Jessica's got, like, a great sense of humor?"

"She does?" Dennis grinned. "I like girls with a sense of humor."

Jessica smiled. "And it's close to April Fools' Day and all," she said, watching little waves bobbing against a buoy. "See, around April Fools' Day, she always likes to pretend she's me."

"Oh." Dennis raised his eyebrows. "You mean—"

"Yeah," Jessica said with a wry shrug. "Jessica likes to call herself Elizabeth. In fact, if you give her half a chance, she'll probably swear up and down that she's really me!"

"I see." Dennis pursed his lips, but Jessica could

see that his eyes were smiling. "Pretty sneaky, huh?"

"So don't believe her if she tries to pull that stuff on you." Jessica winked at Dennis. "Remember, there's only one Elizabeth Wakefield at camp," she said, crossing her fingers behind her back just in case.

"And it isn't my sister!"

Ten

◇

"Don't look now, Elizabeth," Amy said in a soft voice at dinner that evening, "but there's somebody *watching* you over there."

"Really?" Elizabeth frowned. She and Amy were in line, waiting to help themselves to hot dogs, hamburgers, potato salad, and baked beans. A day in the sunshine had made her feel ravenous. "Who is it?"

"Well, it's a boy," Amy said. "He's at one of the tables already. But it's not Todd."

Elizabeth couldn't help craning her neck just a little. "A boy?" she asked doubtfully. "Are you sure he's looking at me?"

"Positive." Amy stared meaningfully at Elizabeth. "There's not, you know, somebody else, is there?"

Elizabeth widened her eyes. "Somebody *else?*"

"Never mind," Amy said with a grin. "OK, he's

turning around. Quick! Over there—the tall blond guy about three people down from Bruce Patman?"

Elizabeth spun around and followed Amy's pointing finger. *Bruce Patman—Bruce—* There was Bruce, all right, complaining that the camp didn't have an all-you-can-eat sundae bar. *Typical.* She counted one guy, two guys, three guys—

Strange. She barely knew the boy Amy was pointing to. Dennis was his name, she remembered. Dennis . . . Dennis Somebody-or-other. "He's, like, a seventh-grader or something," she whispered to Amy.

"I don't know him at all," Amy said. "How do you know him?"

Elizabeth shook her head. "I don't," she whispered. "I think I was walking through the hall once, and somebody said 'Hi, Dennis,' and I noticed him just because he was whistling a Johnny Buck song." She went through the possibilities: he wasn't in any of her classes, he didn't work on the school newspaper, their lockers weren't near each other. "In fact," she said in a more normal voice, "I don't know anything about him at all. Except his first name, I guess."

Amy raised an eyebrow. "Then why was he staring at you?"

Elizabeth shrugged. It was very uncomfortable to be stared at when you didn't even know why you were being stared at. "Maybe I remind him of his long-lost cousin or something," she said.

Amy gave her a funny look. "Somehow I don't think that's it."

They had come to the front of the line. Elizabeth served herself and checked quickly back over her shoulder. Dennis Whatever-his-name-was was looking in her direction again, and when he caught sight of her, his face broke out into a big grin.

It was a nice grin, but it made Elizabeth feel a little weird. Quickly she turned back to the food table and took an extra piece of corn, wishing Dennis had something better to do than to stare at her. Well, she wouldn't let it bother her. Camp was too much fun, and Todd would be along any second now.

Together she and Amy walked over to the nearest empty table and sat down. "There's something so cool about eating at a picnic table, isn't there?" Amy asked, setting her tray in front of her.

"There sure is." Elizabeth picked up her hot dog and took a big bite. Though the weather had gotten a little chilly, it was a total pleasure to be out under the blue sky. "We ought to petition for them to close the cafeteria at school and just put in outdoor picnic tables."

"Hey, yeah!" Amy's eyes grew wide. "Do you think they'd let us?"

Elizabeth smiled and picked up a potato chip. "Probably not," she predicted, "but we can always try . . . right?"

A shadow fell across their table. Elizabeth

looked up, startled. It was Dennis. "Hi!" he said cheerfully, extending a hand.

Frowning, Elizabeth shook it. "You're Dennis, right?" she asked suspiciously.

"You knew!" Dennis winked. "Hey, it's just like she said. Well, I wanted to say hi, that's all." He backed away from the table and flashed Elizabeth a thumbs-up sign. "Catch you later, Jess. Nice meeting you."

Jess! Suddenly Elizabeth figured it out. He thought she was her sister—that was the problem. "I'm Elizabeth!" she called after Dennis, but he was already too far away to hear her.

"Well, I guess that explains it," Amy remarked, chewing on a mouthful of hamburger.

"I guess so," Elizabeth agreed. "He must have gotten to know Jessica somewhere, and now he thinks she's me." She grinned ruefully at Amy. Mix-ups like that happened all the time. "So next time I see him, I'll just let him know who I really am before he runs away."

"Sounds easy," Amy said. "Hey, have you tried the pickles yet?"

"What's the matter?" Lila asked fearfully.

She sat up straight in the dark tent. Either someone was screaming, or else little tiny people were shooting off firecrackers inside her ear. "What's the matter?" she asked again. *Maybe it's a bear*, she thought grimly, and she began to claw her way out of her sleeping bag. *A real bear, not the Aaron-made-up bear from the other night at the campfire—*

"Is everybody all right?" Kimberly played a flashlight around the tent.

Lila shut her eyes to keep from being blinded, but closing her eyes didn't stop the screaming. She grabbed for her shoe just in case she needed a weapon. Her heart was beating furiously. Where were the emergency exits?

"It's Janet!" Mandy cried out.

Lila opened her eyes to see the light jabbing through the darkness and illuminating Janet's tear-stained face. Jessica, Mandy, and Ellen were already out of their sleeping bags. "What's the problem?" Kimberly demanded.

"There was a *spider* in my sleeping bag," Janet sobbed, the words coming out in gulps. "A big fat hairy spider."

"A spider?" Mandy sucked in her breath. "Are you all right?"

"A *spider?*" Lila jumped the rest of the way out of her sleeping bag, fully expecting something big and huge and furry to smother her. "Are you *sure?*"

"It was . . . a spider," Janet said brokenly. "With legs and everything!"

"I knew it," Kimberly muttered. "If I get bitten by a poisonous spider, I want everybody to know that I'm going to sue the camp and the school and anybody else I can think of for a million billion trillion dollars." The light bounced back and forth as she spoke.

"Are you all right, Janet?" Mandy repeated.

"Did you get bitten? Because if you did, we have to get you over to the infirmary right away and—"

"Well—" Janet paused and sniffed. Lila thought she seemed a little calmer now. "I guess—it didn't bite me. Yet," she added, staring around the tent. "It was, like, six inches long, and it sparkled in the light and—" She shivered. "It was totally awful."

"Well, it's gone now," Mandy said. She clicked on her own flashlight. "No spider here that I can see."

"Look harder," Janet insisted. She pulled her sleeping bag up to her chin. "I . . . I . . . I just know I'll have nightmares about it for the rest of my life. If I even live that long. It was so disgusting! Hairy and . . . and brownish yellowish greenish, and it looked up at me and—" Her voice trailed off into a sea of sobs.

Beams of light bounced through the tent. "It's not here," Mandy said, but she didn't sound so certain anymore.

"It's probably just waiting till we all go to sleep," Kimberly said meaningfully. "I for one am not going to lie down in here again until we squash its little head off."

"Me neither," Ellen said shakily. "In fact, I think I see—"

Lila held her breath for a moment, ready to scream.

"Sorry," Ellen said after what seemed like a century. "False alarm. It was just a piece of fluff."

"*I'm* not staying in here with a giant spider," Jessica put in.

"But where else can we go?" Mandy asked. "Not outside. It's raining. And not to the little museum building. It's locked for the night."

Lila tugged at her ear, trying not to make sudden moves that might frighten foot-long spiders with humongous fangs. She swallowed hard. "I guess we're going to have to stay here then," she said. The glimmerings of an idea were coming to her. "Maybe we can—you know, stand guard."

"Stand guard?" Jessica looked at Lila questioningly. "What do you mean?"

"Um—like soldiers in the olden days," Lila explained. "You know, they'd take turns? They'd all sleep except one, and—" There was stuff about passwords, she remembered dimly from last year's ancient history class, but that didn't seem to have much to do with spiders. "And that one would, you know, would take the flashlight and make sure the spider didn't come in."

"It's probably a whole family of spiders," Kimberly pointed out.

"Don't *say* that!" Ellen squealed.

"Make sure the whole family of spiders didn't come in, then," Lila continued. She was proud of herself. It wasn't often that she had a really good idea like this one. "So, um, what do you guys think? Janet?"

There was silence while everyone waited for Janet to think it over.

"Sounds OK to me," Janet admitted after a

moment. "But first everybody needs to shake out their sleeping bags. Just so we make sure, because Lila's idea's pretty dumb unless we do that first, right?"

Pretty dumb? Lila felt her cheeks turning pink. "But—"

"And then Lila will be the first one to guard," Janet continued. "Then Jessica, then Kimberly, then Mandy, and then—um—Ellen."

Lila frowned. "How about you?" she wanted to know.

Janet heaved a long drawn-out sigh. "Number one," she said, "I'm president of the club. And number two, I was the one who discovered the spider to begin with. So I was, like, the first guard."

"But . . ." Lila's voice trailed off. Slowly she stood up and reached for Kimberly's flashlight, trying her best not to step on anything that might be a hairy spider in disguise.

She knew from long experience that there was no use arguing with Janet.

Starvation, Jessica thought bitterly, standing in her accustomed spot by the sign-up board. *Mosquito bites. Poison ivy. Sunburn. And now I'll die from lack of sleep!*

But in order to make her plan work, she had to be up first thing in the morning. Again. Even though she had already been up watching half the night for Janet's spider. If it had ever existed. Jessica had her doubts, but she didn't dare mention them to Janet.

She yawned—and suddenly snapped to attention. Dennis was coming down the path.

"Hi, Dennis," she said, stepping out to block his way. "Um . . . how's it going with my sister?"

"Oh, hi, Elizabeth. She's cute," Dennis said, his face brightening up into a smile. "She really is. You were right, by the way. She looks just like you, only she's lots cleaner and—" He broke off and turned red. "I'm sorry, I didn't really mean that."

"No problem," Jessica said, resisting the urge to tear Dennis limb from limb. She reminded herself that he thought he was talking about her. "You know, I was just, um, noticing," she said casually, tapping the sign-up board, "that Elizabeth, I mean *Jessica*, signed up for tennis."

"She did?" Dennis stooped and stared at the list. "Yeah. But she used your name."

"What a kidder, ha ha ha," Jessica said, realizing that she'd forgotten to change the name on the list. She grabbed the marker and crossed out *Elizabeth*. "Silly old Jess." In quick letters she wrote in *Jessica* instead. "Here," she said, handing the marker to Dennis. "There's still a spot on the board for you. Might want to sign up fast. You know—keep an eye on, um, Jessica."

Dennis nodded. "Maybe I should do just that," he said, and he scrawled his name on the next empty line of the sign-up sheet. Then he turned and gave Jessica a mock salute. "Catch you later, Elizabeth!" he said.

"Have fun!" Jessica told him.

She waited till he was gone. There was still one more thing she had to do. It wouldn't work to have Todd constantly hanging around Elizabeth, especially with those two being so lovey-dovey and all. Watching them would turn Dennis away from Elizabeth—um, Jessica—faster than you could say "Arnold Weissenhammer."

Jessica's eyes sparkled as she scratched Todd's name off the tennis sheet. You could barely read his name under all the ink; it looked as if some kid had signed up and then changed his mind. Now— where to put him?

There were only four activities still open. Empty lines stretched under the title "The History of Bannerman's Estate." Jessica shuddered and moved on. Macramé—Todd had done that yesterday, hadn't he? Forget that. Which left two choices: orienteering and nature study. She wished she knew what orienteering was. At least it sounded relatively safe. Like the kind of thing you might do inside.

While nature study might be walking through thorns and handling snakes and studying insects up close and personal.

With quick strokes Jessica signed her name on the "Orienteering" board.

And added Todd's name directly beneath it.

Eleven

◇

"But I *know* I signed up for tennis lessons," Todd insisted. He stared imploringly at the coach in charge of the tennis courts.

Elizabeth stood by him, confused. "He did," she confirmed. "I was right there. I saw him."

The coach's eyes ran down the sign-up list. "Wilkins," he muttered. "Wilkins, Wilkins, Wilkins—"

"Did you find it?" Elizabeth asked hopefully.

"There's a Wakefield," the coach said. "You're not Wakefield, are you? Can't really make out the first name, but that's the only *W* last name I can find."

Elizabeth sighed. "Wakefield is me." A thought struck her. "Who signed up on the line under Wakefield?"

The coach peered closely at the clipboard. "Fellow named Patman. Bruce or Brice or something.

Actually, come to think of it, there's a name crossed out. . . ." His voice trailed off. "Wilkins, you said?"

Elizabeth's heart leaped. "That's right. Todd."

The coach laughed, a deep guffaw that seemed to explode out of his stomach and into the morning air. "Well, sonny, I'm sorry. Looks like you changed your mind at the last minute."

"But . . . but . . ." Todd looked to Elizabeth for support. "I didn't cross my name out. I wouldn't have done that! We were planning to play doubles together!"

Elizabeth bit her lip. "Couldn't he play anyway?"

The coach frowned. "Well, I'm sorry, miss." He gestured to the courts behind him. "But I can only take sixteen. Four courts, four players on each, sixteen total. And I've got 'em." He patted Elizabeth on the shoulder. "Next time, OK?"

Elizabeth spread her hands wide. "But . . . just because Bruce decided to cross Todd's name off the list . . ." She stared at Bruce, who was already on one of the courts. Holding his racket like a baseball bat, he was smashing balls as hard as he could.

"That really isn't fair," Todd complained.

The coach made noises deep in his throat. "Well, I'm sorry, kids. I guess your friend Bruce is just going to have to live with what he's done." He turned away.

"Todd!" a voice rang out.

Elizabeth spun around and saw her sister coming up, beaming. "What are you doing here?"

Elizabeth asked, taking an involuntary step back. Her sister was looking worse and worse.

"I'm on my way to orienteering," Jessica explained. "And I saw Todd out of the corner of my eye, and I thought I'd—pick him up!"

"Orienteering?" Todd narrowed his eyes. "But I didn't sign *up* for—"

Jessica narrowed her eyes. "Well, your name is on the sheet," she said. "I know because it's, like, right below mine. I mean, above mine," she added quickly. "I saw your name, and so I signed up."

"You—what?" Elizabeth put a protective hand on Todd's arm. Not that she suspected her twin of trying to steal her boyfriend, but something very strange was going on.

"Oh, I didn't mean it that way," Jessica explained with a casual laugh. "I just, you know, really wanted to orienteer, and I'm so psyched to have someone I know in the group!" She yanked Todd's arm. "Come on, Toddster, let's roll!"

Elizabeth stood, frowning, as Jessica led Todd away. Then with a sigh she picked up a tennis racket and headed for the courts.

Yes, something *very* strange was going on. She only wished she could figure out what.

A nice quiet inside thing to do, Jessica repeated to herself, remembering what she'd thought about orienteering earlier that morning.

Ha!

Orienteering, she decided, was the worst possible so-called sport she could imagine. She would rather swim across a river filled with hungry crocodiles than go orienteering ever again. Jessica sat down on a mossy rock to adjust her shoes, which were covered with mud so thick you could barely even see the laces. Gnats buzzed above her head. The forest seemed to stretch on in every direction.

Orienteering. She gave a scornful laugh. The moment the teacher had started explaining it, she knew she'd made a serious mistake, but by then it was too late to change to another activity. It turned out orienteering was trying to find your way out of the woods using only a map and a compass. Even that might have been possible, except that she'd lost the compass in a swamp and the map had been shredded by thorns, so she wasn't even sure which end was up anymore.

She stood up. The gnats made it impossible for her to sit down. Well, if she kept going straight, she'd get somewhere eventually. Right? Watching carefully for snakes, she edged her way forward.

The true definition of orienteering was mud, bugs, thorns, and deer poop. She'd have to write a letter to the dictionary people. *If* she ever got out of here alive.

There was only one consolation, Jessica thought as she slipped on a wet leaf and fell headlong into a tree. Dennis and Elizabeth were sure to be hitting it off over at the tennis court. Jessica smiled to herself.

That almost made the whole orienteering business worthwhile.

"Hey, Jessica!" Dennis greeted Elizabeth, bouncing a ball up and down on his racket. "Want to be my partner?"

"Elizabeth," Elizabeth corrected him absentmindedly. She couldn't stop thinking what a bummer it was to miss out on playing tennis with Todd. "I'm actually Elizabeth."

"Ha, ha, what a kidder," Dennis said heartily. He tossed the ball to Elizabeth. "Here, catch!"

Elizabeth caught it automatically and threw it back. She didn't feel like playing silly games. "No, I really *am* Elizabeth," she said. "Jessica's my sister."

Dennis's lips crinkled into a smile. "Sure, Jessica," he said. "Whatever you say." Whistling a Johnny Buck tune, he shouldered his racket and wandered off.

Elizabeth stared after him, annoyed. And Amy had said it would be easy to convince Dennis he was talking to the wrong girl. But she decided Dennis wasn't worth getting really upset over—especially when she needed to save her energy to chew out Bruce, who was still pummeling the tennis ball.

"Hey, Bruce!" Elizabeth yelled. She strode toward Bruce. Bruce had no business scratching out Todd's name and putting his own name in there instead. The more she thought about it, the madder she got. "Hey, Bruce!"

Bruce gave the ball an overhead smash. It careened crazily off the court and hit the side fence. "What?" he snapped.

Elizabeth took a deep breath. "How come you crossed out Todd's name on the tennis sign-up?" she demanded.

"Huh?" Bruce curled his upper lip. "What are you talking about?"

"You know perfectly well what I'm talking about!" Elizabeth crossed her arms and glared at him. "You crossed off Todd's name so you could write your own. I want to know why you thought you could do that."

"What's your problem?" Bruce made a face. "I didn't cross anybody's name off any list."

"Yes, you did!" Elizabeth hated it when people lied. "You crossed out Todd's name and then you wrote yours right above it, as if you didn't know."

"Whoa!" Bruce took a step backward and held up one hand as if he were warding off a vampire. "I signed up late, you got that part right. But I didn't cross off anybody's name. I looked at the list real close," he added, jabbing a thumb at his chest. "And there was one space where someone had crossed himself out. So I wrote myself in." He stared at Elizabeth.

"Oh." Elizabeth's shoulders slumped. She hadn't expected this response. She'd guessed Bruce would either proudly admit it or make up some story about how he'd been the first one to sign up.

"Todd's name was already crossed out? Are you sure?"

Bruce snorted. "Sure, I'm sure." He wiped sweat off his forehead. "Look, I'm sorry if Wilkins didn't make it into this class, but it's not my fault, OK?" He bounced off without waiting for an answer.

Elizabeth frowned. She almost believed him.

But if Bruce was telling the truth, then how had Todd's name gotten off the tennis list and onto the orienteering one?

A ball soared through the air and came to a stop at her feet. "Hey, Jessica!" Dennis called, cupping his hands to his mouth. "How about a little help, huh?"

"So how's it going?" Jessica asked Dennis that night at the campfire. It had taken her about six days to get out of the woods, during which time she had been tempted to eat the roots and berries she found there. Except the roots were hard and woody and buried three feet underground, and the only berries were the kinds that were usually poisonous. She never had figured out how people in books did it.

Dennis shrugged. "Fine, I guess. You were right, by the way. She keeps telling me she's Elizabeth." He curled his lip at Jessica. "Of course, the way you look right now, I can't imagine why."

"You'd think she'd be old enough by now to give that up," Jessica said, doing her best to ignore his last comment. "Of course, she's a really cool kid in, like, every other way," she added hastily, just in case Dennis might decide Elizabeth/Jessica was too weird to keep pursuing.

"She *is* pretty cool," Dennis admitted. "Good-looking too. But there's one thing I want to know. Who's that kid over there with her?"

Jessica blinked. Elizabeth was sitting practically in Todd's lap. At least it looked that way from where she was sitting. "Oh, *him*," Jessica said brightly, stalling for time. She wondered how to handle this.

"Yeah, *him*," Dennis said meaningfully. "They look kind of close. And you said she had a crush on me." He frowned at Jessica. "I don't want to be, you know, horning in where I'm not wanted, if you catch my drift."

Jessica's mind raced. "Oh, Todd won't mind" didn't seem like the right response somehow. And "He's our brother" obviously wasn't going to cut it. She considered saying that Todd was just a momentary crush for "Jessica" and that by next week she was sure to be over him. But as she opened her mouth, she suddenly had another idea.

She'd tell the truth. Sort of.

"Todd?" she said with a casual grin. "Oh, Todd's really my sort-of boyfriend. He just likes to hang around with Jessica sometimes and try to make me jealous."

"*Your* boyfriend?" Dennis made a face. "*You* have a—"

"Well, I'm not usually this disgusting!" Jessica shot back. "Camp just doesn't agree with me. Anyway, ask anybody. They'll tell you. Todd Wilkins and Elizabeth Wakefield are really, you know." She shrugged and winked slyly at Dennis. "An item."

Dennis took a deep breath. "Well, OK," he grunted. "So Todd's not, like, interested in her. I guess you'd know the truth, huh? Since you know Jessica better than almost anybody else does?"

"You could say that." Jessica tried not to laugh.

And actually Dennis's question had made her a little nervous. She knew she'd have to work harder to keep Elizabeth away from Todd if her plan was ever going to succeed.

"Elizabeth?" Todd asked later that evening. "Do you get the feeling there's somebody following us?"

Elizabeth halted in the darkness. She could hear nothing but crickets chirping and the occasional hoot of an owl. The path she and Todd were walking on was completely deserted. The stars overhead shone like flashlight beams poking through black construction paper. "No," she admitted, gripping Todd's hand tightly. "Do you hear something?"

"Footsteps," Todd said, narrowing his eyes. "But I can't see anybody. Can you?"

Elizabeth shook her head. This hadn't been exactly the day she'd planned on. First there had been the mix-up about the tennis sign-up sheet.

Then, when all the kids had been at the campfire and she and Todd were just beginning to get close to each other, Jessica had appeared out of nowhere and plunked herself down between them. And now, when she and Todd were finally having their romantic walk beneath the pines, somebody or something was following them.

"There *is* somebody," Todd said after a moment. "Listen."

Elizabeth listened again. Now she could hear it. And what's more, she could see it. A flashlight beam bobbed along in the darkness, bouncing rapidly up and down. "Hey, guys!" called a familiar voice.

Elizabeth's heart sank. *Jessica.* "What do you want?" she asked irritably.

The light caught up, and now Elizabeth could see her sister's blotchy face. "I've been looking all over for you!" Jessica gasped. "Do you have any idea what time it is?"

"Time?" Elizabeth stared at her sister and felt for her watch, but she'd left it back at the campsite. "No, I don't, Jess."

"It's about eight-thirty." Todd's grip tightened on Elizabeth's arm. "Come on, Elizabeth."

"I was afraid of that." Jessica clutched her chest and panted dramatically. "Do you have a watch?"

"No." Todd sounded curt.

Jessica sighed heavily. "Oh, man, I don't believe it. Boy, am I glad I found you."

"What are you talking about?" Elizabeth stared at her disheveled sister. "We have until nine o'clock before we have to be back at our tents. That's the rule. It was even on the information sheet and everything: Campers have to be at their campsites precisely at nine—"

"But don't you *see*?" Jessica cried out anxiously.

Elizabeth threw Todd an exasperated look. "Jessica, would you please do us a favor and go away?"

"I can't!" Jessica sounded panicked. "It's too late! See?" And she thrust her wrist so close to Elizabeth's eyes that Elizabeth had to step back to see it. "Look what time it really is!"

Elizabeth's eyes grew big as she saw the green numbers lighting up on her twin's wristwatch. 9:42. *9:42!*

"Uh-oh." Todd let go of Elizabeth's hand, and his jaw dropped open slowly. "We're in trouble now."

Elizabeth felt a sinking sensation in her stomach. "But it can't be!" she argued, not sure whether to believe her own words. "We couldn't have been out for—" When had they left? About eight? "For a whole hour and a half! No possible way!"

But Todd didn't say anything. Elizabeth bit her lip. What if they truly had lost track of the time? What if time really did fly when you were on a romantic walk with your sort-of boyfriend. . . .

Jessica seemed to read her mind. "Follow me, Lizzie," she suggested earnestly. "I think I can smuggle you in through a crack in the fence. If we're lucky . . ." She hesitated. "*If* we're lucky," she emphasized, "no one will find out."

Elizabeth could only nod. Waving Todd a quick good-bye, she followed Jessica. The flashlight bobbed on the path in front of them, turning this way and that. Elizabeth breathed a sigh of disappointment.

She only hoped she wouldn't get into too much trouble.

The walk had been romantic, all right. But it wasn't worth getting into trouble over.

"*What* time did you say it was?" Elizabeth demanded.

Jessica tried to sound innocent. "Well, according to my watch, it's just about exactly 9:53." She rested her arm against the nearest tent. "Why, Lizzie? Is something wrong?"

Elizabeth looked murderous. "It isn't 9:53, you doofus! It's 8:53!" She gestured at the kids still milling around the entrance to the girls' camp. In the crowd Jessica recognized Bruce Patman, Ken Matthews, and a few other boys from her grade. "We had more than fifteen minutes left, Todd and me, and you—" She clamped her mouth shut and shook her head angrily. "And you had to go and ruin it!"

"Hey, take it easy," Jessica said, backing up just in case her twin decided to ruin *her*. "It can't be 8:53," she insisted, holding her watch up to her ear. "It says 9:53. No, 9:54 now. And it's still lighting up and everything."

"Then how do you explain this?" Elizabeth advanced a step. "If it's really practically ten o'clock, why haven't all these kids been caught? How come they aren't all in trouble?"

"I . . . I don't know." Jessica hoped she sounded convincing. "Maybe they, like, changed the rules?"

Elizabeth sat down on a rock. "Oh, go away," she said crossly. "I'm tired of you, Jessica! Fix your watch and just leave me alone!"

Jessica felt momentarily guilty. She knew how much her sister had looked forward to walks in the woods with Todd. But there was no way around it: Getting Dennis to notice her was more important. And if Elizabeth spent too much time with Todd, then Dennis might lose interest. "I'm sorry, Lizzie," she said, spreading her hands wide. "I just can't imagine what happened to the watch."

Besides being set forward an hour, that is!

Elizabeth sighed. "I know it was a mistake, Jessica," she said, not quite looking her sister in the eye. "But you know, weird things have been happening all day long, and you always seem to be right in the middle of them."

"Me?" Jessica had expected a comment like this. She put her hands on her hips and glared hard at her sister. "Well, if you think I had any reason to—"

"No, I don't." Elizabeth rubbed her eyes. "But it's—" She paused. "It's almost as if you're interested in Todd or something. It's like you're pushing me away from him because you want him for yourself instead." She shoved a lock of hair out of her eyes and stared directly at Jessica. "We're sisters, Jess, and I won't put up with that kind of stuff if you're going to be sneaky about it. So tell me." She leaned forward and spoke seriously. "Are you interested in Todd?"

"Me? *Todd?*" Jessica practically choked. "Absolutely not!" And for a change, she reflected, what she was saying was the complete truth.

Twelve

◇

"Oh, man," Ellen moaned. "There's sap in my hair, and it won't come out."

"You think you've got problems." Jessica snorted. "After that orienteering yesterday, my body will never be the same. Even my bruises have bruises."

It was Wednesday morning. Lila had been awakened, as usual, by Charlie Cashman's grunts and squeaks on the trumpet. Only this time she hadn't been able to get back to sleep again. Neither had the other Unicorns.

"There were at least three cockroaches in my sleeping bag last night," Janet announced. "At *least* three. I got, like, two minutes of sleep."

Mandy sniffed the air delicately. "I think we should all take showers," she suggested.

"No way am I taking a shower in water that

looks like barf!" Janet turned a withering stare on Mandy. "And I'm not stinking up the place, like *some* people I could mention. Right, Ellen?"

"I don't stink!" Ellen sniffed her armpit just in case.

Lila suspected that Ellen didn't smell any worse than Janet. But she decided not to say so. An idea was beginning to play in her mind.

"If I ever hear the word *camping* again, I'll probably murder the person who said it," Kimberly announced.

"I'll *definitely* murder the person who says it," Janet agreed. "And not just the word *camping* either." Her eyes glittered. "Other words too. Like *tents*."

"And *spiders*," Kimberly put in. "And *sleeping bags*."

"And *sap*," Ellen muttered.

"And *campfires*," Janet said contemptuously. "No offense or anything to the idiots who dreamed this trip up, but this was without a doubt the dumbest, stupidest idea for a field trip *ever*."

"Then—why don't we just leave?" Lila sat up straight, suddenly excited.

"Leave?" Jessica stared at her. "We can't just leave!"

"Why not?" Lila plucked a burr off her leg. *Why not indeed?* The more she thought about it, the more sense it made. "If we don't like it, let's take off," she said casually. "I'll call Daddy's voice mail. He checks it, like, eight times a day. Then he'll call back, and I'll have him send Richard with the limo. I can stay with one of you guys till Mrs. Pervis gets back."

Mandy frowned. "I don't think it'll be that easy, Lila," she said.

"I don't see why not." Lila shrugged. "I usually get my way, you know."

"At home, yeah," Ellen said slowly. "But at school it's different. Remember the time when you tried to get out of that science lab by saying you had to—"

"That has nothing to do with it," Lila interrupted quickly, waving her hand. "The school doesn't run this camp, it just rents it. If I say I'm Mr. Fowler's daughter, the camp people will, like, fall all over themselves to do what I want."

"Good idea for once, Lila," Janet said. "I appoint you and Mandy to go make that call right now. And Lila?"

Lila jumped up. *Sweet Valley Mall, here I come!* she thought jubilantly. "What is it?" she asked.

Janet smirked. "Just make sure Richard brings the really *big* limo. The one that holds all of us."

"I'm going to watch this board like a hawk today," Todd said on Wednesday morning. His gaze flicked across the sign-up lists. "And if that Patman, or anyone else, tries to scratch me off again . . ."

Elizabeth smiled uncertainly. "So, um, what do you want to sign up for?"

"Let's see—" Todd scanned the titles of the activities. "Tennis might be fun," he said brightly.

"No good." Elizabeth shook her head. "I did it yesterday, and you're only allowed to do it once."

Todd frowned. "Here's a trip to an old abandoned silver mine. That might be kind of cool."

Two hours in a smelly old bus. "No, thanks," Elizabeth

said with a shudder. "How about—um—this one?" She pointed to "Intermediate Basket making." "Maybe we could, like, work together?"

"Yeah," Todd said thoughtfully. The marker scurried across the sheet. "Maybe we could."

"What do you mean I can't use the phone?" Lila demanded, staring down her nose at the woman behind the desk. "Don't you know who I am?"

The woman sighed and adjusted her glasses. Lila guessed that she was probably the camp secretary. "I know exactly who you are," she informed Lila. "You're a camper, and the rule is, no outgoing phone calls except in case of an emergency."

"Come on, Lila," Mandy muttered from her side. "Let's just leave."

"I am Lila *Fowler!*" Lila took a step forward. "The daughter of Mr. George Fowler, of Fowler Enterprises? You know, the company that makes, like, practically everything?" Why wouldn't this woman see reason? "I *demand* to make a phone call right now!"

The woman's eyes narrowed. "Don't you use that tone with me, young lady," she said. "I don't care if you're the queen of Spain—the rule says no phone calls, and that goes for everyone." She swiveled her chair and faced a computer keyboard.

Lila bit off a retort. Beyond the woman's head she could see the telephone, friendly and inviting. A lifeline to freedom. "Please," she wheedled.

"That isn't going to get you anywhere either,"

the woman remarked without looking up. "Rules are rules."

"But it *is* an emergency," Lila protested, switching quickly to another strategy.

The woman looked up suspiciously. "What?"

"Um—" Lila thought hard. The woman probably wouldn't believe that her dad's helicopter had just been wrecked in the Alps. And "I was supposed to baby-sit my little brother all week" wouldn't cut it either. She fingered her greasy, smelly hair. "Well, if I don't get a real shower in, like, the next three hours, it'll *be* a real emergency!" she said.

The secretary rolled her eyes. "Sure," she said. "Listen, I've got tons of stuff to do today, so if you don't mind—" She nodded meaningfully toward the door.

"I knew it," Mandy whispered.

Lila drew herself up to her full height and stared angrily at the secretary the way she always did with incompetent salesclerks. "Ma'am," she said icily, "I'm afraid I shall have to report your rudeness to your supervisor." *There*, she thought with satisfaction. *That ought to get her.*

"Go ahead," the woman invited Lila. "Since I don't have a supervisor." She sat back in her chair, folded her arms, and looked Lila directly in the eye. "I don't believe we've met officially. But I'm pleased to make your acquaintance. My name's Dolores Sanchez, and I'm the camp director."

*   *   *

"Hi, Dennis." Jessica intercepted Dennis as he was about to sign up. "How are you?"

"Hi, Elizabeth," Dennis said, sniffing the air delicately. "Um, I'm fine—how are *you?*"

"Fine," Jessica said brightly, though in truth her stomach was hurting a little. "Listen, um—are you still interested? In my sister?"

Dennis shrugged. "Sure, I guess," he said. "It's pretty much the same as last night. She hasn't been, like, noticing me very much or anything."

Jessica smiled to herself. "Yes, she has!"

"Really?" Dennis frowned.

"Well, you're signed up for the same activity as she is," Jessica told him, pointing to the basket-making list.

Dennis looked—then looked again. "Basket making?" he muttered. "I didn't sign up for this."

Jessica felt a surge of irritation. "I know, duh," she said before she could stop herself. She tapped the name above Dennis's. "This is the one who did it."

"Oh!" Dennis's eyes widened, and his lips began to curve into a grin. Above his name was written "Jessica Wakefield."

"So don't say she's not interested," Jessica admonished him. "She just shows it in funny ways."

Dennis nodded. "I guess she really likes me," he crowed. He clapped Jessica across the back. "Hey, thanks a million for telling me that, Elizabeth," he said. "I was about to sign up for, like, orienteering instead!"

"Well, I'm glad I stopped you," Jessica said,

smiling. "Signing up for orienteering would have been a really bad idea. Believe me, I know!"

"So what do we try now?" Ellen asked.

"I don't know," Lila admitted, staring up at the ceiling of the tent. She'd come so close to actually leaving camp, she didn't think she could face another night here. "But we've got to do something."

"But *what?*" Ellen insisted.

"We've got to think." Kimberly set her jaw. "Why would they let kids go home from camp early?"

"If there was, like, a disaster or something," Mandy suggested. "Maybe we could pretend there was an earthquake. Or a volcano."

Janet waved the idea away. "It would never work," she scoffed. "They'd turn on CNN, and that would be the end of that."

"Maybe if there was, like, a movie out that we absolutely had to see?" Ellen ventured.

Lila sighed impatiently. She couldn't imagine trying that line with the camp director.

"Homesickness," Kimberly said.

"That might work." Janet nodded. "Or—real sickness." Her eyes lit up.

"Real sickness?" Lila shook her head violently. "No way am I getting really sick." She'd been sick before. Running back and forth to the bathroom got old real fast.

Janet smiled slyly. "We could be really sick

without actually getting really sick." She looked around the tent. *"If* you catch my meaning."

Pretend. Of course! Lila grinned. "You mean like this?" She clasped her hands to her stomach. "Ohh," she moaned, settling back and doing her best to turn a shade of pale green.

"Ohh," Kimberly and Ellen echoed her.

"If we *all* do it, they'll think there's been one of those epidemics," Janet said. "And they'll send us all home. Everyone's here, right? Everyone except for Jessica?"

"Ohh," Mandy groaned.

Lila looked around. Jessica was gone again. *Some Unicorn!* she thought, concentrating on looking truly ill. "Ohh," she murmured.

"Sounds good," Janet said approvingly. "Only look like you're really about to barf. Stick your tongue out and make gagging noises. Like this." She demonstrated.

"Aggh-aggh!" Lila swallowed hard. Noises like that made her actually want to throw up. "Ohh."

"And you know, we really *could* all be sick," Janet said. "With the water and all."

Lila had forgotten about the water. She thought about drinking a glass of that horrible stuff. Her stomach flip-flopped. "Ohh," she gasped.

She almost didn't have to act anymore.

"Hi, Jessica!" Dennis greeted Elizabeth at the basket-making workshop. "How you doing? Want to be my partner?"

Elizabeth frowned. "I'm really Elizabeth, Dennis," she said for what felt like the millionth time. Maybe she ought to wear a sign that said "I'm Elizabeth." "I'm not kidding or anything."

Dennis's mouth crinkled into a smile. "Sure, Jessica," he said with a wink. "So, how about it? Want to be partners?"

Elizabeth scratched her head. Dennis really seemed like a nice guy, but she was planning to work with Todd. Plus she had no interest in Dennis, and it wasn't fair to let him go on thinking she was someone she wasn't. "The problem is—"

"I thought so." With a grin Dennis steered her toward one of the workstations, where reeds and tools were lying out in the sun. "Don't worry, Jessica," he said, "I won't talk to you much or anything."

Elizabeth cast her eye around for Todd. "But there's somebody—" Her voice died away when she saw that Todd was walking in the opposite direction, looking confused.

And being led by her very own sister.

"So let me get this straight," the camp nurse said doubtfully. Tall and thin, she wore a tag that said her name was Wendy. Her eyes flicked from one Unicorn to the next. "*All* of you are sick?"

"Ohh," Lila moaned, clutching her stomach.

"Ohh," moaned Janet and Ellen and Kimberly and Mandy. They sprawled across the floor and chairs of the infirmary, looking as pathetic and as sick as they possibly could.

Wendy frowned. "You don't have a fever, girls," she said gently.

"We've been in and out of the bathroom all morning!" Janet gasped, coughing violently. "Mostly in."

Ellen groaned louder. "I feel like my insides are about to come out," she rasped.

"Really," Lila added. On a cabinet she noticed a coffee mug that said, "If only one of you is sick, why are there seven of you in my office?"

Wendy held a thermometer up to the light and shook it. "People aren't usually this sick with a normal temperature," she said.

Lila willed herself to sweat. "I—I read about it in *Health and Beauty Secrets*," she said, her head lolling back. "It's, like, a killer virus from South America or Sweden or one of those places. You don't ever get a fever, but you die anyway."

"Please, send us home!" Kimberly begged. "If you don't, probably the whole camp will get infected."

"Hopefully it isn't already too late," Ellen said between retches.

Wendy rubbed the side of her head. "Well—let me ask a couple of questions, girls," she said. She sat down at her desk and pulled out a black three-ring binder. "Which side of your stomach hurts the most?"

"The right side," Ellen said.

"The left," Kimberly said at the same exact moment. They turned to look at each other.

Uh-oh, Lila thought.

"The right side!" Ellen repeated, clutching the right side of her stomach.

"OK, the right side," Kimberly said hastily. "Actually, like, the whole thing." She covered her mouth and leaned against the back of her chair. "Water," she croaked.

Wendy looked at her thoughtfully. "Is it a burning pain or more of a needle kind of pain?"

"Needles!" Lila shouted, hoping to get out an answer before Ellen could speak.

"Burning!" Janet sang out.

Lila swallowed hard. "Well, both, actually," she admitted in a strangled voice. "More burning than needles, I guess."

"It's so hard to tell," Mandy said, breathing hard. "Sometimes it's one and sometimes it's the other."

"I see." Wendy stood up. "One more question. Who was the first one of you to throw up this morning?"

There was silence. Lila twisted uncomfortably, waiting for someone else to speak so they wouldn't contradict each other. *Just don't say it was me*, she begged her friends silently. She would be too embarrassed.

Kimberly cleared her throat. "Ellen was."

"I was not either!" Ellen sat up straight and glared at Kimberly. "You take that back! Lila threw up before I did."

"Yeah, and worse too," Janet said. "It was, like, all over her clothes."

"No, I didn't!" Lila leaned forward. "That was, um—" She tried to figure out who wouldn't mind. "Mandy."

"Yeah, Mandy," Ellen said.

"Yeah, Mandy," Kimberly echoed.

The room was silent again. The Unicorns all turned to look at the nurse.

"Like I said," Wendy told them. Her eyes smiled behind her wire-rimmed glasses. "It's very unusual to have a terrible stomachache without a fever. And it's obvious that this isn't one of those times." She sat down at her desk. "Back to camp!"

"I hate to say it," Dennis whispered, leaning close to Elizabeth as he worked, "but your sister looks like she's crawled out of a rat's nest—know what I mean?"

Elizabeth sighed. "Jessica doesn't usually look that bad," she said, pushing a reed into place. Her mind was whirling. Nothing was making any sense. Bruce Patman wasn't even here in this workshop, so he probably didn't have anything to do with what was going on, and Jessica had sworn she had no interest in Todd, and of *course* Todd didn't have any interest in Jessica, so—

"You mean Elizabeth." Dennis applied some glue.

Elizabeth sighed again. This time she didn't even bother to correct him. What was the use? She stole a quick glance at Todd and Jessica. Jessica was talking up a storm, Elizabeth could tell, although she didn't think Todd was paying any attention.

"It's weird." Dennis reached for a new reed. "It's like she's living her life through you or something, the way she's pushing me onto you."

Elizabeth stiffened. "The way what?"

"Oh, nothing." Dennis shrugged. "She and that Todd guy seem pretty close, though."

Elizabeth adjusted her collar thoughtfully. The sun had gone behind a cloud bank some time ago, and it was a little chilly. "Oh, yeah," she agreed, setting her jaw. "Elizabeth and Todd go way back." Her brain struggled to fit in this new piece of the puzzle. *If Dennis and Jessica have been talking . . . and if Dennis seems absolutely positive that I'm Jessica . . . then . . .*

"I saw you with him too," Dennis said. He bent over their basket and tugged. "For a minute I thought this was, like, sisters going for the same guy. But Elizabeth told me it wasn't like that at all." He laughed. "If it was, it'd be like that story that Egbert told. Remember, the other night? About the twins? The one who switched places with her sister?" He laughed again.

The sun peeked out from behind a cloud. "I remember," Elizabeth said.

She stared across at Jessica, who had turned to look at her and Dennis. But when she saw Elizabeth's gaze on her, Jessica turned away.

Elizabeth smiled grimly to herself.

Suddenly it was all starting to make sense.

Thirteen

◇

"Hey, Egbert!"

Aaron stood at the edge of the dock. He waved his arms frantically, trying to attract Winston's attention.

"Egbert!"

In the little red canoe halfway across the lake, Winston Egbert stuck his paddle into the water. The boat lurched forward so quickly, Winston nearly fell overboard.

"Eg-*bert!*" Aaron cupped his hands and shouted as loudly as possible.

Awkwardly Winston lifted the paddle out of the water and stuck it in again. He pulled hard toward the side of the boat. Little waves washed against the canoe, and Winston swung his arms wildly in the air to keep his balance.

Winston was not exactly the world's best paddler,

Aaron decided irritably, watching as Egbert's canoe veered crazily from one side to the other. Every two or three strokes Winston changed sides, ducking his head out of the way except when he forgot.

"Earth to Winston Egbert!" But Winston didn't even turn around.

Aaron sighed, and his shoulders slumped forward. He wouldn't usually have cared much about what Winston the Egghead did with his life, but now he really wanted his attention. There was a very important job Aaron wanted him to do.

Aaron still remembered the incredible rush he'd gotten at the campfire that night when everyone had been scared out of their wits. The time when he'd told them there was a bear. What an incredible feeling of power!

He smiled to himself, remembering the way they'd screamed, the way they'd scattered. The look on Bruce Patman's face! And the way Jessica's mouth had opened into a perfectly round O of surprise . . .

He felt just a little bit guilty about Jessica, to tell the truth. It hadn't been exactly nice to scare her that other time. And then to laugh. But he'd make it up to her.

It wasn't like there was anyone else she was going to go after.

Out on the lake Winston dipped his paddle into the water, stroked hard, and clouted himself in the jaw with the top end. Aaron winced.

He had a plan, a plan to scare them all again. A plan to make them believe there truly was a bear.

All he needed was a little preparation.

And a little help from Winston Egbert.

"So I was, you know, just wondering," Todd said softly. Basket making was over, and it was almost time for lunch. "I mean, it's none of my business and all, but—"

"You're wondering about Dennis, aren't you?" Elizabeth said. She felt for her half of their lucky four-leaf clover, nestled safely in her pocket.

Todd hesitated. Then he took a deep breath and plastered a smile onto his face. "Yeah," he admitted. "I've just been . . . you know, noticing that you guys have been spending . . . a lot of time together."

Elizabeth took a deep breath. "Well, it isn't my choice, I'll tell you that," she said wryly. "Listen, Todd. Have you noticed that Dennis thinks I'm Jessica? And that Jessica looks like—" She paused, wondering how she could put this delicately. "Like yesterday's newspapers?"

"Yeah." Todd frowned. "So?"

"That isn't just a coincidence," Elizabeth said. "Here's what I think is going on. Jessica wants Dennis to notice her. But this is a terrible week for that, right? She won't take a shower and, well, outdoor living isn't her thing."

"You can say that again." Todd rolled his eyes. "But what does this—"

Elizabeth held up a finger. "So being Jessica, she hatches this incredibly complicated plan," she went on. "She tells Dennis I'm Jessica. Then—"

"I get it," Todd said slowly. "And he sees you, and he gets interested because you're so—" He blushed, and his eyes dropped. "Well, you know."

Elizabeth couldn't help blushing herself. Then she cleared her throat. "So he's been following me around, thinking I'm Jessica," she said. "Jessica must have told him that I like to pretend to be her." She marveled at how sneaky her twin could be. "So by now he's hooked—on someone he thinks is Jessica Wakefield."

"And next week," Todd continued grimly, "when Jessica's back at school—"

"All combed and clean," Elizabeth supplied.

"—she'll go after him for real and pretend you were her all along." Todd scratched his neck and grimaced. "It's not like she consulted you, did she?"

Elizabeth shook her head. "It would have been nice," she said.

"And you could have said no," Todd argued. "Now it's like our week is ruined. I'd hoped— well." He paused. "Never mind. But it's like I keep looking up everywhere I go to see if Dennis is about to pop out at me. At *us*." He pulled his lips into a tight, thin line. "There ought to be something we can do to get Jessica back."

Elizabeth smiled. Her fingers tightened on the clover in her pocket. She'd been thinking the same thing all morning, and she had finally come up with a plan. "Actually," she said, hooking her elbow into Todd's, "there is."

"Come quick, come quick, come quick," Lila mumbled to herself over and over. She sprawled on her smelly sleeping bag in her smelly tent, smelling the smelly smells of the smelly Unicorns nearby. "Come quick, come quick, come quick. I am in terrible trouble, terrible trouble, terrible trouble . . ."

"Mom, Dad, this is serious," Kimberly chanted next to her. "Mom, Dad, this is serious. Come at once."

"You miss me soooo bad," Ellen muttered, barely moving. "Come pick me up now because you miss me soooo bad. . . ."

It was practically lunchtime, but none of the Unicorns cared. Lila took a deep breath and began again. "Come quick, come quick, come quick," she hissed, wondering if thought waves could reach all the way to Rangoon or wherever her dad was today. *Well, if telephone wires could, why not thought waves?* Kimberly's idea that they all send urgent ESP messages was definitely a good one.

"Your little daughter needs you." Janet stared intently at the top of the tent. "I mean, you need your little daughter—"

"I am in terrible trouble," Lila went on. Was it better to vary the words of the message a little, or was it better to stick with the same thing? Lila rolled over. *Stick with the same thing,* she decided.

There was less chance for a mix-up that way.

"This is so cool," Mandy murmured. "I feel like I'm actually in contact with my mom. Do you think I'm psychic?"

"Shhh!" Janet said from her sleeping bag, and Mandy was quiet.

I don't know about you, but I'm definitely psychic, Lila thought as she recited the words under her breath. It was a really weird feeling, she decided. There was something—electric in the air. As if her dad was trying to get through to her too. For a second she tried to make her mind a complete blank, hoping to catch whatever message he was sending. But all she could hear was the murmuring of the other girls.

"You miss me soooo much," Ellen was saying. "Soooo much . . ."

There was a sudden sound at the flap of the tent. Lila sat up straight, her heart beating furiously. "Daddy?" she croaked, scarcely able to believe her good fortune.

"Huh?" Jessica, looking pale, came into the tent. "Guess what! Dennis and Elizabeth were actually *smiling* at each other during—"

"If you don't mind, Jessica," Janet interrupted sarcastically, "some of us are trying to send ESP messages to our parents?"

"Yeah, it's, like, a life-and-death situation?" Lila was disappointed that it wasn't her dad after all. But then, Rangoon was a long way away. "Like, if we don't get home soon, we die?"

Jessica swallowed hard. "But during basket making—," she began weakly. "Dennis Asher and Elizabeth were—" She paused. Her eyes snapped shut for a moment. "Smiling at each other!" she finished triumphantly, before she collapsed back against her pillow.

"How nice for them!" Janet snapped. "Now shut up and let's keep going. 'Oh, Mom and Dad, you need your beautiful, strong, and smart daughter so badly, and not just so she can dry the dishes and take out the garbage once in a while . . . ,'" she intoned solemnly, closing her eyes.

"Oh, Dennis, I'm so glad to see you!" Elizabeth gushed. She batted her eyelashes at Dennis in what she hoped was a Jessica sort of way, and she squeezed in next to him at his lunch table.

Gag! she thought dismally. But it was all for a good cause, she reminded herself. All to benefit the Make-a-Fool-of-Jessica Foundation.

"Hi, Jessica!" Dennis smiled broadly. "I'm really glad to see you too."

"I was noticing how you were kind of looking at me during basket making," Elizabeth purred. "So does that mean what I think it means?" She leaned closer to Dennis and fixed her lips in a brilliant smile.

If Jessica wants Dennis to fall for me, she thought, *I'll make him fall for me, all right! He'll fall so hard and so fast, he'll never know what hit him.*

Or who!

Dennis groped for his fork, but he didn't take his eyes off Elizabeth. "Well—," he said gingerly. "Um—what do *you* think it means?"

Elizabeth had her answer. "Isn't this so cool, the way we met?" she said. "I mean, I came to camp and I'd never really seen you before. And now I have! And I'm really glad." Elizabeth nodded emphatically. "And you know what's *really* cool?"

"What?" Dennis lifted one eyebrow.

"It's just like—like there was this *force* that brought us together!" Elizabeth reached for his hand. "Don't you think so?"

"Oh, cut it out, Jessica," Janet said impatiently. "You're not sick."

"And we already tried it," Lila went on reproachfully. "The nurse is too smart for that. She won't let you go home."

Jessica squeezed her eyes shut. Her bones ached, and her head felt two sizes too big. "I'm—I'm not faking," she blurted, but the voice seemed to come from far away.

"Yeah, right." Janet sounded contemptuous. "Stop pretending."

"It's not like you've been around a lot lately or anything," Kimberly added. "If you'd only been here, you'd have known that—"

Jessica opened her eyes and tried to focus on her friends' faces. But the tent was too busy spinning. She shut her eyes as Ellen's face dipped toward her.

Her stomach was spinning too, spinning at least as fast as the tent, if not faster. She tried her best to swallow, but something else seemed to be coming up the other way—

There was a moment of silence, and then a horrible noise.

"Oh, yuck," Kimberly said. "Ellen, go get some paper towels."

"Like, *lots*," Janet agreed, holding her nose.

"It's all over my *sleeping* bag!" Lila cried angrily. "I absolutely do not believe it! She got it all over my sleeping bag!"

Despite how terrible she was feeling, Jessica couldn't help smiling inside.

"I told you I was sick," she managed to croak before collapsing against the wall of the tent.

"So—um, Dennis?"

Elizabeth bit her lip as she and Dennis crossed in front of the nature center, hand in hand. She wasn't really crazy about holding hands with a guy she didn't *like* in that way, but she had to do what she had to do. "There's something I, um, need to tell you," she said softly.

"Yeah?" Dennis frowned. "What is it, Jess?"

Elizabeth was almost getting used to being called by her sister's name. She and Dennis had been hanging out for almost three hours now, ever since lunch, and Elizabeth was more than ready to slip off with Todd for a few minutes. Or preferably more. She smiled faintly. "Well, you know that I've got a twin sister. Elizabeth."

Dennis nodded.

Elizabeth's hand stroked her clover. She smiled, thinking of Todd. "Elizabeth's kind of funny," she said, searching the forest floor for exactly what she needed.

"You're telling me," Dennis said with feeling. "I mean, talk about nuts! She'd make some family of squirrels very happy."

Elizabeth plowed on, trying to remember that Dennis was really talking about her sister. "One of the things she likes to do," she went on, "is pretend she's me."

"That's funny." Dennis leaned against the nature center. "Because *she* said that *you* liked to pretend you were her."

"Well, who are you going to believe, me or her?" Elizabeth demanded. Actually, she reflected, Dennis's comment pretty much proved what Jessica had been up to. "Anyway, it can be hard to tell who's who sometimes."

"Not as long as she looks like *that*," Dennis muttered.

Elizabeth stooped and picked up a beautiful red maple leaf that had fallen from a nearby tree. She folded it along the middle seam and tore it gently in two. "Hang on to this," she told Dennis, handing him half of the leaf and thrusting the other into her pocket alongside the half clover.

Dennis looked questioningly at Elizabeth.

Elizabeth laughed, hoping she sounded casual. "Just in case," she said. "You know, if we're back at school or something, and she tries to pass herself off as me?"

Dennis grinned and waved the leaf in the air.

"That's right." Elizabeth smiled back. "This way you'll always be sure which one of us is really which!"

Fourteen

◇

"What are we now, oh-for-three?" Kimberly asked. It was later that afternoon, and the Unicorns were sitting underneath a huge oak tree. Their tent still smelled like Jessica's barf.

"Well, first we tried calling home, and that didn't work," Mandy said. "Then we played sick—"

"And that didn't work." Janet's eyes flashed. "Thanks to some people whose initials are Ellen Riteman."

"And then the ESP didn't work either," Lila said dejectedly. Three tries, three strikes. It looked as if they'd never get out of this place. She watched in disgust as five gigantic ants lurched crazily across the ground.

"We don't know that hasn't worked yet—," Ellen began.

Kimberly cut her off. "If it hasn't worked by now, it'll never work," she said. "Luckily for all of you, I have an idea. An idea that will actually fly," she added.

Lila jerked her knee up so the ants wouldn't climb onto her leg. "What is it?"

"There's another way to get home from camp," Kimberly said. "A foolproof way. Listen. *Let's break all the rules*."

Mandy gasped. "Break all the rules?"

Kimberly nodded triumphantly. "There's no detention room here. So what will they do with us instead?"

"Send us home, of course," Janet said slowly. The corners of her lips turned upward. "Great idea, Kimberly."

"I don't know," Mandy said slowly. "I mean, if we really broke *all* the rules, they'd probably call our parents. And we'd be grounded. Maybe even suspended from school for a while."

"Every party has a pooper—that's why we invited *her*." Ellen made a face and pointed at Mandy.

Kimberly waved her hand impatiently. "Well, we don't have to break *all* the rules. Just a couple."

"Tell you what," Janet suggested. "We'll stage a fight." She sat up straight, a gleam in her eye. "It'll be, um, Mandy and Lila and Ellen against me and Kimberly, and me and Kimberly will be winning, of course, and we'll throw lots of punches and maybe get some ketchup to use as fake blood."

"Yeah, and we could say it was just that camp made

us, like, crazy," Lila put in. The more she thought about it, the more sense the idea made. The only thing she didn't like was that Janet's side would be winning.

"Can't I be on your team, Janet?" Ellen whined.

"No." Janet put her arm around Kimberly's shoulders. "So how about it, Mandy? If you're not interested," she added darkly, "well, there's a couple of other sixth-graders who might be interested in joining the Unicorns. . . ."

Mandy's eyes flashed with alarm. "All right," she said after a moment. "Count me in."

No mosquitoes. No snakes. Four strong plaster walls. Jessica knew she should be thrilled to be away from the tent at last.

Unfortunately she was too sick to enjoy it.

"Hmm." Wendy pulled a thermometer out of Jessica's mouth and stared at it. "This isn't good, Jessica. Your temperature's very high."

Jessica nodded weakly. Even that little motion made her dizzy. She could see Wendy's long dangling earrings glisten in the harsh light of the infirmary. That sight made her dizzy too.

"I could give you something to bring the fever down," Wendy added, as if thinking aloud, "but I'm not sure you'd be able to keep it in your stomach. Which means . . ." She sighed.

Jessica hated it when people sighed at her. She lay still, sweating on her cot, feeling as if she'd never move again.

"Well." Wendy set down the thermometer and made some notes on a chart. "We'll keep you here overnight for sure, and then we'll see."

Overnight for sure. "So I'm, like, really sick?" Jessica asked, but she suspected she already knew the answer.

Wendy picked up her coffee mug and sipped from it. "I guess you could say that, Jessica," she confirmed. "You're, like, really sick!"

"Ladies." Ms. Sanchez, the camp director, folded her arms and stared solemnly at the Unicorns in front of her. Despite herself Lila quaked a little as the director's steely eyes brushed across her own. "The Bannerman Estate has some *very* clear rules, which you and your parents read *and* signed, and the most important of all is—?" She paused expectantly.

"No staying up late?" Ellen guessed.

Lila rolled her eyes. "No fighting," she said.

"Correct." Ms. Sanchez leaned forward, her mouth a tight line, and she tapped her foot impatiently on the ground. "To be quite honest with you," she said, "that's a rule that boys tend to break, not girls."

"We're sorry, Ms. Sanchez," Kimberly said. "We don't know what got into us."

"I guess it was just being cooped up in a smelly old tent," Janet said. "Most of the time we're really friends."

"Yeah," Lila added. "We'll never do it again, I

promise!" It might only have been a pretend fight, but Janet's kicks and scratches had left a few marks on her arms and neck. And the way Kimberly had grabbed her from behind and pushed her into the big oak tree hadn't *felt* very pretend. Her cheek still ached from the rough bark.

"What she *means*," Janet said, "is that we *probably* won't do it again."

"But you can't be sure," Kimberly hastened to add. "So I guess you're going to have to punish us, huh?"

Lila did her best to look miserable at the thought of being punished. She held her breath, hoping to hear the magic words—*I'm sending you home.*

"Of course you'll be punished." Ms. Sanchez flipped through a notebook. "Let's see. The grease trap in the kitchen needs cleaning. You will all be responsible for doing that before dinner tonight."

The grease trap? Lila stared in astonishment. She'd seen grease traps before: big jars under stoves where all the gobby, gloppy, gluey grease collected after cooking. "Clean it out?" she gasped.

"But—but that's not a punishment!" Janet half rose from her seat.

"No?" Ms. Sanchez said calmly. "Have it your way. Clean out the grease trap tonight *and* tomorrow night." She stood up. "A pleasure doing business with you ladies. Let's try not to meet again, shall we?"

"But—" Kimberly leaped to her feet. "I thought you were going to do something—else. Like, send us home?"

"What would be the point of that?" Ms. Sanchez curled her lip. "That's a total cop-out. If you're having trouble, the thing to do is to keep you here and work on it."

Lila's mouth felt dry. "But—," she began.

"This way you have to clean out that grease trap as a team," Ms. Sanchez told them. "Which means you have to learn to get along. For a change. *Understand?*" She narrowed her eyes. "That means, 'Got it?'"

"Got it," Mandy mumbled.

"What if we refused to empty out the grease trap?" Lila swallowed hard. "What if we just, like, went on strike?" If they refused to do the job, they'd have to be sent home—right?

"Yeah," Ellen added. "Then what?"

A smile played at the corners of Ms. Sanchez's mouth. "Well, ladies," she said, "how do you like getting to choose what to drink at mealtimes?"

Lila stared at her friends. "Um—," she said.

"Because," Ms. Sanchez said, "the only drink I'm required by law to give you is water. Everything else is a luxury." She folded her arms again slowly. *"Understand?"*

Lila could practically taste the disgusting water. A shiver ran through her. When it came to swallowing her pride or swallowing the water, it was an easy choice.

"Understand," she said sadly, and she stood up to lead the way to the grease trap.

*   *   *

"So we're going to spend a *lot* of time together tomorrow, right, Dennis?"

It was dinner that night, and Elizabeth was actually almost having fun pretending to be Jessica. She leaned closer to Dennis. "A *lot*. Right?" she repeated.

"Um—yeah." Dennis licked his lips, then broke into a smile. "Yeah. I'd love to, Jessica."

"We'll sign up for all the same things," Elizabeth continued. "And we'll have lunch together. Dinner too."

"OK." Dennis swallowed his milk.

Was it Elizabeth's imagination, or was he edging away? She leaned closer still.

"Of course," she whispered huskily, practically in his ear, "there are times I'll just have to get away for a while, even from you. Like today." She'd had a short swim with Todd that afternoon. Even getting back at Jessica wasn't as important as spending time with Todd. "OK?"

Dennis nodded. This time Elizabeth was sure that he was edging away. "What's the matter, Dennis?" she asked sweetly.

"Oh—nothing." Dennis managed a faint grin. "It's just that—well, your sister said you were kind of, you know, shy."

Elizabeth put her hand to her chest in mock horror. "Shy? Oh no, Dennis! Shy is one thing Jessica Wakefield definitely is *not!*"

*   *   *

Several tables away, Aaron pushed away what remained of his fried fish and coleslaw. Under the bill of his LA Dodgers hat, he studied the two figures intently.

The guy was Dennis Asher. That was for sure.

And the girl was either Elizabeth or Jessica, that was definite. The only question was which one. He could have told for sure if they were closer, but they were way across the field from him. Unfortunately he had a sneaking suspicion that he knew which one it was.

The girl leaned even closer to Dennis.

"Hey! Hey, Aaron!" Winston Egbert poked his ribs. "About tomorrow night—"

"Shut up, Egbert." Aaron didn't turn to look at Winston. He narrowed his eyes, weighing the evidence.

Elizabeth wouldn't throw herself on some guy like that.

Plus, Aaron could see the rest of the Unicorns sitting at a table nearby, and Jessica wasn't with them.

Plus, Aaron dimly remembered hearing Dennis talk about some really cute girl he'd met named Jessica. . . .

Gently he rubbed his jaw, thinking dark thoughts. If that was really Jessica, he had a problem. A *big* problem.

He'd have to keep a careful eye on Dennis from now on.

Fifteen

"So how are you feeling this morning?" Wendy asked.

Jessica's only answer was a groan. She was burning with fever. Every bone in her body ached. Even her eyes didn't seem to focus right.

"Oh, dear." Wendy bent down and touched Jessica's wrist. "Your pulse is unusually fast," she murmured in a voice filled with concern.

Jessica shut her eyes and tried to stop the world from spinning. "Am I going to—need—a shot?" she asked. Her jaw felt like a block of wood.

"I don't think so," Wendy reassured her. "But I think your own doctor should have a look at you."

"My own—doctor—" Jessica struggled to sit up. Her eyes flicked open, and she gazed into Wendy's face. Or rather Wendy's faces; there were at least three of them. "But that means—"

"What's your telephone number?" Wendy asked, seating herself at the desk and lifting the receiver. "I hate to say it, kiddo, but I'm sending you home."

"This is *it*," Janet hissed, staggering out of the kitchen after the Unicorns' second night cleaning the grease trap. "This is positively the *end*."

Lila looked at her hands, wondering whether to laugh or to cry. They would never be the same again. Globs of grease clung to her fingers, and her thumb would smell like old bacon bits for weeks. "It's the end, all right," she said with conviction. "I will *never* in my entire *life* clean a grease trap again, no matter what."

"That's not what I meant." Janet's voice was firm. "I mean we're not hanging around here any longer. It's the end of this camp for us."

"But what else can we do?" Ellen whimpered. "We've tried everything already."

"We haven't tried everything," Janet corrected her. "There's still one way out."

"We could wait for the bus," Mandy suggested. "It's Thursday already, and it leaves on Saturday. That's only two days."

"Two days of misery." Kimberly glared at Mandy.

Lila made a face. "I can't wait for the bus," she said.

"No way am I waiting for the bus," Janet said loftily. "I'm a woman of action, and I say we need to *do* something. Did you see Jessica?"

Lila pushed back a wave of jealousy. She *had* seen Jessica being loaded into her mother's car for the wonderful drive back to Sweet Valley. Jessica had looked pretty sick, she had to admit, but Lila would have given up a lot to take her friend's place. Three of her Belle da Costa swimsuits. Or two of them anyway.

"We're going to run away," Janet announced.

"Run away?" Ellen frowned. "How would we do that?"

"Easy," Kimberly snapped. "Put one foot in front of the other?" She demonstrated. "Of course, it's harder for some of us—"

"Look." Janet's eyes glittered. "It can't be that hard. It's not like they have an electric fence around the estate. And there are roads all over the place. I mean, this is *California*. Three hundred zillion million people live here, right? How far before we get to a police station or a kind lady?"

"Or a trucker with a cell phone?" Kimberly put in.

"Or a *shower?*" Janet finished.

Lila took a deep breath. It sounded awfully good. "I vote yes," she said.

"Me too." Kimberly's hand shot up.

"How about wild animals?" Ellen asked. "I don't want to be trudging through the woods after dark when you might step on snakes and stuff—yuck."

"Then we'll take flashlights," Janet snapped. "We'll go tonight. We'll just kind of sneak away from the campfire and then—" Her eyes gleamed. "Hot shower, here we come!"

Aaron looked right and left. No one was around.

He eased open the door of the nature museum. "Hello?" he called softly.

No one answered.

Heart beating furiously, Aaron edged through the open door. His eyes took a moment to become accustomed to the gloom. Though he'd never been in the museum, he'd been in other ones like it, and he was positive they had what he needed.

Let's see, he thought nervously, walking around the empty room. *A stuffed wildcat . . . a bunch of mushrooms . . . leaves—aha!*

Quickly Aaron's arm shot out. The bearskin was heavier and furrier than he had expected, but it would do, all right. In fact, it was just about perfect. It even smelled like a bear.

Aaron stuffed the skin into his backpack and was disappointed to see a few stray hairs hanging out. *It's not like I'm going far*, he reminded himself. He started to walk out the door—but stopped suddenly.

Someone was coming.

Aaron shoved the backpack quickly under a bench. He hoped they wouldn't come in. Whoever they were. Ducking, he leaned against the door and peered out.

His heart sank. Coming down the trail were Dennis Asher and someone who looked very much like Jessica.

"Oh, Dennis," the girl was saying. She giggled in a Jessica kind of way and clung to Dennis's arm. "I sure hope you still have the other half of that maple leaf I gave you!"

Dennis winked at the girl as Aaron watched in dismay.

"I sure do, Jessica!" he said, and he pulled out half a leaf from his pocket.

He called her Jessica. So it must be true. Aaron's thoughts were in a whirl. Jessica looked great. A lot better than she had earlier in the week. Suddenly he felt incredibly jealous. What right did Dennis have to take away his sort-of girlfriend? Even if he did play a couple of practical jokes on her. Was this any way to pay him back for that?

They were gone. Aaron hefted his backpack onto his shoulder and strolled out of the nature center, hoping no one could see the bear fur sticking out of the pack.

He was going to have to do something about this Jessica situation.

Just as soon as this little practical joke was over anyway.

This is it, Lila promised herself. Her heart was hammering. The campfire blazed, and the air was full of kids' voices singing happily about the wreck of the ship *Titanic*. But Lila barely listened. Before long the Unicorns would be history too.

She only hoped nobody would notice them

leave. Or get suspicious because they had dragged so much stuff to the campfire. The Unicorns had decided that they couldn't leave any clothes behind, so they'd packed everything but sleeping bags.

"Kerplunk. It sunk. The end. Amen," the kids sang, and Bruce and Charlie added a final "cha-cha-cha."

"Ladies and gentlemen!" Winston bowed extravagantly. "Back by popular demand, it's Winston the Magnificent!"

"Ten minutes," Mandy hissed to Lila. "Right in the middle of his story, OK?"

"I'm here to tell you about the ghost bear of the Bannermans!" Winston said loudly. "The bear that comes out every Thursday night. Gee—what day is it?" He gazed stupidly at his watch.

"Thursday!" the kids chorused.

"Uh-oh." A dark shadow spread across Winston's face. "We might see it tonight."

As if, Lila thought scornfully. But she couldn't help shivering. She looked off into the woods, the dark, empty woods. For a moment she wondered if the ghost bear might actually be a true story.

But only for a moment.

Come on, Egbert, come on, Aaron urged Winston silently. It was hot cooped up in the bear suit, and there were mosquitoes buzzing around his head where he lay hidden in the woods. *Get to the good part.*

He strained to listen. "The bear was not dead," Winston said, his voice floating eerily across the grass to Aaron's hideout. "It reared up on its hind legs and let out a roar that could be heard halfway to Oregon."

Aaron tensed, ready for his cue. He had to hand it to Egbert, the kid knew how to tell a story. "The old miner knew then that he should never have hurt the bear," Winston continued softly. "But it was too late now. His knife shot forward, and the bear fell to the ground. The miner noticed that its eyes would not quite shut."

Aaron grinned. Leave it to Egbert to put in a little detail like that.

"And ever afterward the miner could not sleep on a Thursday, no matter how hard he tried," Winston went on. "The ghost bear was after him. And what's more, no one at the Bannerman Estate could sleep either, not on a Thursday."

Aaron held his breath.

"Even today the bear still walks the hills." Winston paused. "And tonight, if you look very closely, you might even see—"

Aaron stood up. With an angry roar he bolted from the thicket toward the campfire, toward Winston's hand, which was stretched accusingly in his direction. . . .

The screams were the best he'd heard in years, he thought happily.

"Well, how was I supposed to know it was Aaron under that bearskin?" Lila snapped. She lay in her smelly sleeping bag, her stomach still doing flip-flops. "I mean, from a distance it looked like a bear."

Janet sighed with exasperation. "If you'd looked closely, Lila—"

"Well, all of us ran," Mandy pointed out. "And lots of other kids too."

Lila didn't like to relive the terrifying moment when the ghost bear had burst out of the forest. "It was really scary," she said. "And everybody fell for it."

"Not me," Janet insisted.

Which explains why you were running around screaming like a headless chicken, Lila thought irritably. She snuggled deeper into her sleeping bag and tried not to breathe.

"It doesn't matter." Mandy sighed. "The point is, we were all too afraid to run away through the woods after that. Let's just wait for the bus, OK?"

"No way," Janet said scornfully. "We're leaving. Tomorrow, right before dinner."

Lila nodded. Running away while it was still daylight made some sense. Not only that, tomorrow was Friday.

Which meant there wouldn't be any ghost bears.

Deep down she knew that Winston and Aaron had made the story up.

Still . . . she wasn't taking any chances.

Sixteen

◇

"So let me get this straight. Who's the girl you're hanging with all the time?" Aaron called.

It was Friday morning, and Aaron had just cleaned out the grease trap. ("So one stupid bear joke wasn't enough?" Ms. Sanchez had asked him sarcastically before handing down his sentence.) He'd barely stepped outside the kitchen when he'd seen Dennis Asher walking along, looking moony. "Hey, Asher!" he said when Dennis didn't look up. "You! I'm talking to you!"

"Oh, hi, Dallas." Dennis stopped short. "Sorry. What'd you say?"

Aaron gritted his teeth. "I *said*, who's the chick you've been talking up?"

Dennis looked surprised. "You mean Jessica? Jessica Wakefield, that's her name. Man, she sure is hot," he said dreamily.

Aaron coughed loudly. "It might interest you to know that she has the hots for *me*," he said. Didn't the guy know enough to keep his mitts off somebody else's sort-of girlfriend? "So maybe you could, like, butt out?"

Dennis focused his gaze directly on Aaron, as if he had discovered some new and interesting animal. "Jessica? Has the hots for *you?*"

"Yeah." Aaron put his hands on his hips. "Want to make something of it?" He tried to look menacing, flexing his muscles the way Arnold Weissenhammer did in the movies.

Dennis shrugged. "I always figured a girl could choose the guy she wanted, know what I mean? And now if you'll excuse me—" He stepped forward.

"There's no excuse for you," Aaron said forcefully, standing his ground. Who did this guy think he was anyway? "What'd you do—brainwash my girlfriend?"

Dennis took a deep breath. "If you don't mind," he said slowly, taking another step forward so his chest was almost pressing up against Aaron's, "I'm heading for the volleyball court, and I'd like to get there in time to play a game. So if you'd just, like, move aside—"

Aaron knew he probably should do what Dennis wanted. For one thing, Dennis was a little taller than he was and looked a little stronger too. But he couldn't help himself. "I'm not moving," he said stubbornly, "until you give me back my—"

But he never finished the sentence. Instead he stumbled into a tree trunk. "So Jessica had the hots for you, huh?" Dennis asked, dusting off his hands on his pants. "Well, it doesn't look like she's got the hots for you anymore, if you catch my drift."

Aaron rubbed the place on his forehead that had collided with the tree. "But you—I—she—"

"Face it, Dallas," Dennis said, striding off down the trail.

"You aren't exactly the hottest thing on wheels right now!"

"You got rid of Dennis?" Todd asked.

Elizabeth nodded. "I told him we needed a little time apart," she said happily, taking Todd's hand. Together they climbed into a canoe.

"And you're not worried he'll see us?" Todd wanted to know. He stroked powerfully. The boat shot forward.

Elizabeth smiled. "He said he was going to play volleyball. So we're home free." She caught Todd's eye.

"Well—um, here's to us," Todd said shyly, turning around and paddling harder.

"To us," Elizabeth echoed him. She dipped her own paddle in the water and let it trail along. Little ripples split into two long lines and drifted off across the still surface of the lake. Elizabeth breathed deeply.

Fresh air. Beautiful water. A warm breeze. Gentle clouds. Birds in the sky.

And a canoe ride with Todd.

What could be better?

"If we're going to skip dinner, we ought to raid the kitchen for food," Ellen suggested. It was nearly dinnertime, and the Unicorns were finalizing details for their escape.

"Good idea, Ellen," Lila said. "Cookies and cake and maybe some soda pop." She licked her lips. There was no telling how long they'd be stuck out in the middle of nowhere, and she for one was not about to starve to death.

"And candy bars," Janet put in. "Don't forget the candy bars."

"I still don't understand why we don't just wait for the bus," Mandy complained. "I mean, it's less than twenty-four hour—"

"Shut up, Mandy," Kimberly snapped. "If I have to stay one more night in that tent, I'll go stark raving crazy."

"I might die," Lila added. "Or else get incredibly ugly; one or the other. I can just feel my beauty slipping away." She could too. Last night she had huddled so close to the unbarfed side of the sleeping bag that she'd woken up with a crick in her neck, which meant that she'd been walking around all day with her head tilted to one side. Not to mention the canoe ride she'd taken, when she'd fallen into the lake, which she was sure was full of toxic waste—

"As president of the club," Janet announced, "I appoint Mandy and Ellen to get us food for the trip."

"Just come back with something good, guys," Kimberly said meaningfully.

Lila nodded. "Like a lemon meringue pie!" she suggested. She felt a surge of excitement as Mandy and Ellen picked up their backpacks and headed for the kitchen. If all went well, they'd be out of this place in a couple of hours.

And then it would be shower time.

Lila smiled to herself. She couldn't wait.

Aaron sat on a log, debating whether to go to dinner or not. On the one hand, he was hungry. On the other hand, he didn't want to face Dennis after what Dennis had done to him outside the kitchen.

On the *other* other hand, maybe he should go have it out with Jessica. On the *other* other other hand, he didn't want to even *see* Jessica if she was going to hang on to Dennis like she'd been doing.

"It's all Asher's fault," he grumbled. He picked up a stick and sketched "Down with D. A." in the dirt. It made him feel better, so he drew a heart with the initials J. W. and D. A. and erased it with a quick motion of his foot. "It's all his stupid fault." *And maybe Jessica's, for hanging with him instead of me—*

Aaron sighed. The woods seemed awfully empty. *Or maybe it was Winston Egbert's fault for agreeing to tell that stupid story. The one that got me into trouble. . . .*

He swallowed hard. It was more fun to blame other people. But he couldn't escape the nagging suspicion that maybe the fault was his own. Kind of.

Well, a little tiny bit his anyway.

The dinner bell rang, but Aaron made no effort to get up. "Dennis Asher is a jerk," he wrote in the dirt. "And an idiot. And a fool." *There. That ought to show him—*

Aaron froze. Someone was talking. Quickly he erased what he'd written just in case it was Dennis, and he jerked his head up.

" . . . four bags of marshmallows should do it," he heard a familiar voice say. *Kimberly Haver. One of Jessica's best friends.* Aaron peeked around a tree, wondering if Jessica was with Kimberly. But he could see only Kimberly and Janet Howell, walking gingerly across the muddy trail with bulging backpacks.

"I wish my suitcases weren't so heavy," Lila Fowler complained. Aaron could see her coming around a bend, weighed down with a suitcase in each hand.

"It's your own fault," Janet observed. "Nobody told you to bring everything you own on this stupid trip."

"I did not either bring everything I own!" Lila snapped. "I only packed four swimsuits and six pairs of shoes—"

Aaron stifled a laugh. He watched the rest of the Unicorns follow behind Lila. Correction: the rest of the Unicorns except for Jessica. *That*

Dennis! Now he was even taking her away from her friends too!

"I sure hope this works," Mandy remarked.

"It'll work, all right," Kimberly said cheerfully. "Won't they be surprised when they find out we're gone!"

Gone? The girls disappeared around a bend. "What is this, a jailbreak?" Aaron muttered to himself.

The idea was appealing. Slowly he edged out from behind the tree.

Dinner could wait.

Right now he was going to follow those girls.

"We should go left here," Ellen said.

"No, right," Kimberly contradicted her.

Lila stood with a suitcase in each hand, wishing they would figure it out quickly so they could just keep on going. They'd been in the woods for what seemed like hours, and she was beginning to get nervous.

It wasn't the mosquitoes, or the mud, or the increasing darkness. No. It was a feeling that somebody—or something—was following them.

"Go right?" Ellen glared at Kimberly. "That would take us back to camp, Miss Go-in-a-circle!"

"Oh, yeah?" Kimberly glared back. "For your information, we've been going left ever since we started. If we don't go right soon, we might as well just turn around!"

"We really should hurry." Mandy cast an anxious eye at the sky. "Did anybody bring a flashlight?"

Lila looked at Janet. Ellen looked at Lila. Mandy and Kimberly looked at each other.

"Typical," Janet said softly. She shouldered her backpack. "As president of the club, I make the decision. We go left." She led the way off into the gathering gloom.

Sighing, Lila strode along after her. Her arms ached, and the mud on the trail pulled at what was left of her shoes.

And footsteps were definitely sounding behind her. . . .

Aaron frowned. Were those stupid Unicorns stopping *again?* Trust that dippy Lila to bring along way too much to carry. Not to mention, he was certain that they were heading the wrong way. *If they're really aiming for the road*, he thought with a smirk, *they should just keep going straight.*

Ahead of him Lila gave a sharp intake of breath.

Then there was silence.

Probably a really gross caterpillar, Aaron thought, edging closer. He rolled his eyes. *Girls.*

"Oh, man," Mandy said softly. Aaron could see her backing toward him. "Oh, man. That isn't what I think it is—*is* it?"

A megagross caterpillar? Aaron's curiosity was aroused. He took another step. Now he could see the top of Ellen's head.

"Be very quiet." Kimberly's voice was shaking. "Maybe it won't notice us."

Something crashed in the bushes. "Run!" Janet screamed. "It's a bear!"

A bear? Aaron took an involuntary step back as the girls, shrieking horribly, dashed toward him. Then he stopped. *Don't be fooled, you doofus,* he told himself sternly. *They're just trying to get you back. They knew you were following them, and if you run, they'll laugh themselves sick.*

There was only one thing to do. "Hey, where are you going?" he demanded as Ellen flashed past.

"A bear!" Ellen screamed. "A real live bear—big and brown with horrible eyes—" She pounded out of sight.

Aaron raised his eyebrows. He wouldn't have thought Ellen had that much imagination. "Yeah, right!" he called over his shoulder.

The other Unicorns dashed by. "Wait for me!" Lila called frantically.

"Run, Aaron!" Kimberly cried. "Save yourself!"

"You think I was born yesterday?" Aaron scoffed. "There's no bear!" Casually he walked forward past Lila's suitcases. "Here, bearie bearie bearie!" he called. There was nothing to worry about. Nothing at all. "Good bear—"

He stopped short.

Dead ahead was a real live bear. Big and brown with horrible eyes, just as Ellen had described it, standing on Janet's suitcase.

With an awful noise the bear pounced. . . .

"Help! A bear!" Aaron dashed for the nearest

tree. He felt the hot breath of the bear on his back as he grabbed a branch and hoisted himself up.

I should have known, he thought, his heart pounding. *Lila Fowler would never dump her suitcases for any practical joke!*

"Maybe it wasn't a bear after all," Mandy said.

"Maybe it wasn't," Lila agreed. She sat on a log, gasping for breath. They'd been running for at least five minutes, and the bear hadn't appeared. "Are we sure we really saw him?"

"I *know* I saw him," Ellen insisted. "He was big and brown and dangerous!"

Kimberly scratched her ear. "It was getting dark, and we were all kind of scared. At least Ellen was."

"I was not!" Ellen glared at Kimberly.

"I only ran because Ellen said to," Janet pointed out.

"Me too." Lila wondered if she'd only seen a trick of the light. "But what about Aaron?" she asked uncertainly. "He went in after it, and he hasn't come back out."

"Oh, Aaron." Kimberly's eyes flashed. "We all know about Aaron and bears."

"Yeah," Mandy agreed. "I wouldn't put it past him to make the whole thing up. Just to trick us."

Lila nodded. That made sense. "It sure was funny the way he suddenly showed up behind us," she said.

"It sure was." Janet looked grim.

There was silence. In the distance they could hear Aaron's faint voice shouting, "Help! A bear!"

"Well, he's not going to fool *us* again," Kimberly said decisively.

"No possible way." Lila cleared her throat. "Listen, it's pretty dark, and I'm kind of hungry. What do you say we go have some dinner before it gets too late?"

"Isn't that Aaron's voice?" Todd asked.

"Mm-mm," Elizabeth said dreamily. It was later that night, and she and Todd were strolling along a path. The trees glistened in the moonlight. "I think so. Why?"

"Oh, no reason." Todd stopped near a tall pine. "He's shouting, that's all."

Elizabeth strained to hear. "He sounds like he wants help," she said lazily.

"Yeah." Todd stepped closer to Elizabeth. "I think he's yelling about bears."

About bears. Good grief. "Does he think we were, like, born yesterday?" Elizabeth groaned. "I mean, how many times is he planning to play this stupid joke?" She wound her arm around Todd's waist.

"I know what you mean," Todd said. He looked directly into her eyes. Elizabeth's heart gave a leap. "Let's just ignore him, OK? Sooner or later he's bound to give it up."

"Mm-mm," Elizabeth said.

She tilted her head to the side, forgetting all about Aaron.

And Todd's lips pressed quickly against her cheek.

"Somebody, anybody!" Aaron screamed. "Help!"

They couldn't be that far away, he thought. They *couldn't* be! Terror seized his heart. What if nobody heard him?

"Help, help, help, a bear!" he cried again, but his throat was getting sore, and the words didn't travel as far. He'd been treed for at least an hour. "Call 911, a bear!"

But the only reply was the sound of heavy breathing at the foot of the tree.

Bears can climb trees, right? Aaron was already about thirty feet up, clinging precariously to a misshapen branch. But what if thirty feet wasn't enough?

"Help!"

Taking a quick look down, he shuddered.

In the moonlight the bear's eyes looked like two red coals of fire.

He began to climb even higher.

Seventeen

Just a bad virus, the doctor had said. *In a couple of days she'll be just fine.*

Well, Jessica thought happily on Saturday morning, *he was right!*

She sprang out of bed, feeling better than she'd felt in a long time. Her bones didn't ache anymore. Her head wasn't throbbing. Her forehead didn't feel hot, and the room wasn't spinning.

Now to get all the rest of the woods out of her system. Jessica could hardly wait.

First she'd take the longest shower ever. Lava soap for the poison ivy and about three whole bottles of shampoo for her hair. Then she'd practically roll in cream and lotion until every one of those hideous scabs and scratches was soothed. Next a visit to the hairdresser's. A curling iron. A little makeup.

And finally she'd head for school to watch the buses come in. Just as glamorous as a movie star.

She smiled and headed for the bathroom.

If she couldn't wow Dennis after the beauty treatment she was about to give herself, well, he was unwowable. That was all there was to it.

"Some April Fools' Day," Mandy groaned. She hoisted her suitcases onto the back of the bus and climbed in herself.

"You said it." Lila felt too tired to cry. The Unicorns had spent their last night at camp without any comforts at all. They hadn't dared to retrieve their luggage till morning. Lila had been forced to sleep in her smelly clothes, and even her toothbrush was gone. Everything had been left out near Aaron and his mythical bear.

"It will take me months to recover from this," Ellen moaned. "My hair is never going to be the same again."

"Mine either." Kimberly plopped down in the seat next to Lila's. "There's only one person on this whole bus who looks worse than us."

"One person?" Lila frowned. She couldn't believe anyone had suffered more than they had. "Who's that?"

Kimberly stabbed her forefinger toward the front of the bus. "The boy who cried bear," she said dryly. "Aaron Dallas himself."

Lila drew in her breath. Aaron did look horrible.

His skin was bruised in places, and there were dark circles under his eyes. Plus, twigs and leaves were hanging on to his clothes, and the imprint of a piece of bark was visible on his cheek. Almost as though he'd spent last night in a tree, she mused.

Not that he would have done anything so totally stupid, of course.

"Man alive," Aaron said crossly. He folded his arms. "I sit there in the tree the whole stupid night and what happens? Nobody comes to get me."

Winston raised an eyebrow. The bus pulled through the camp gates, horn honking. "I heard you yelling for help," he said. "But I wasn't falling for it."

"Falling for it?" Aaron demanded belligerently. "What do you mean, falling for it? This one was *real*," he insisted, holding out his arms as if to demonstrate just how big the bear was. "It treed me, I'm telling you! Its eyes glowed all night, and I hardly slept a wink—" He broke off. "Why are you looking at me like that?"

"Admit it, Dallas." Bruce rolled his eyes. "You were just waiting for us all to come and 'rescue' you."

"So you could jump out of the tree and holler, 'Gotcha!'" Dennis Asher put in. "Personally, I don't think that was very smart. Or very mature."

Great. Aaron shoved his hands into his pockets. "Well, why do you think I look like this anyway?" he snarled. "What do you think—I spent the night in a tree for my health?"

Charlie Cashman snickered. "You probably climbed up and then right back down," he said. "Hey, guys, I've got a riddle. What football team scares the living daylights out of Aaron Dallas? I'll give you a hint—it isn't the Dallas Cowboys!"

"The Chicago *Bears!*" Dennis answered, laughing.

Aaron longed to punch Dennis in the nose. "So where's your new *girlfriend*, huh, Asher?" he asked through clenched teeth.

"Jessica?" Dennis grinned. "She's on the other bus. Said she needed a little time to herself."

Good, Aaron thought. A feeling of sadness welled up inside him. For the first time he really regretted having been sort of mean to Jessica. *Jessica would have stuck by me*, he told himself. *Jessica would have stroked my back and said, "I believe you about the bear, Aaron."* Jessica would have told the others off about making fun of him. *Jessica— Jessica—Jessica—* If he concentrated hard enough, he could almost hear the engine of the bus singing out her name.

"What did Aaron say when he saw a bear for real?" Bruce began to chuckle.

"What?" Winston asked.

"*Bear*-ly anything!" Bruce doubled over with laughter.

Aaron wished Jessica was with him now. He missed the feeling of her hand in his. And he hated to think of her with Dennis, the rat. He only hoped it wasn't too late. Maybe there was something he could do to get her back. . . .

"Hey!" Winston burst out excitedly. "When Aaron met an animal in the woods and it wasn't wearing clothes, what was it?"

"What?" Dennis asked.

"A bare bear!" Winston shouted, slapping his knee.

Sheesh. That's not even funny! Aaron settled back and groaned.

It was going to be a long trip back to Sweet Valley.

"Well, I had a good week," Todd said softly. He turned to Elizabeth, sitting next to him on the seat. "Did you, um, have fun too?"

Elizabeth reached for his hand. "I had a wonderful time," she said.

"Good." Todd's face relaxed. They looked into each other's eyes, enjoying the moment.

And I did have a wonderful time too, Elizabeth thought, dropping her gaze at last. She shut her eyes tight, trying to paste all the pieces of the week into the scrapbook of her memory. The pine trees swaying crazily in a stiff wind. The smell of bacon in the morning sunshine. The sensation of bare feet in the grass outside the nature center. The sound of waves lapping against the canoe she shared with Todd.

And the feel of Todd's quick kiss against her cheek, under the moon that last night.

Elizabeth's eyes flew open again. "A wonderful

time," she repeated. She reached for her half of the four-leaf clover in her pocket.

Hey. Had it brought her luck, or *what?*

"Hi, there," Jessica said seductively. She flashed Dennis a smile as he got off the bus, making sure to show him her newly brushed teeth.

"Hi, Jessica!" Dennis grinned back. "You're looking better than ever. How was the bus ride, huh?"

"The bus ride?" Jessica's heart thumped loudly in her chest. She hoped not loudly enough for Dennis to hear. "Oh, well, you know. Like a bus ride!"

"So, um, you want to go get some pop or something?" Dennis asked cheerfully. "My folks are picking me up, but since the bus got in early—"

"Sure!" Jessica's heart soared. "I'm, you know, sorry I was a little standoffish at camp," she said. "I just like being on my home territory a little better is all." She giggled nervously. In the background Aaron got off the other bus. He looked awful. *Good thing I'm through with him,* she thought. *Dennis is much cuter!*

"Standoffish?" Dennis blinked. "Boy, Jessica, if that was standoffish, I'd hate to see what you're usually like!"

Jessica wondered what he was talking about. "Well, let's go," she said brightly, pulling him away from the buses before someone spilled the beans about who she really was. "It's time for us to get to know each other now."

"Now?" Dennis narrowed his eyes. "What are you talking about, Jessica? We already got to know each other pretty well, didn't we?" He winked. "Remember the walk in the woods? Our dinner together? We've had some pretty special times together already."

"We have? I mean, oh, yeah!" Jessica corrected herself. *Walk in the woods? What walk in the woods? And when did we eat dinner together?* Her mind strained to figure out what was going on.

"Yeah, that dinner," Dennis said. He grinned wolfishly and licked his lips. "Like, all the different kinds of pizza in the whole entire world. Sausage, and pepperoni, and mushroom . . . and the company was pretty good too."

Jessica decided she'd better get with the program. "Oh, yeah, those pizzas were unbelievable," she agreed. *Pizzas?* she thought anxiously.

Dennis sighed. "Especially the pineapple," he said, as if he could actually taste it. "The best I've ever had."

Jessica grinned. Now she was on solid ground. "Oh, yeah, that pineapple one!" she agreed with feeling. "My all-time favorite too."

Dennis frowned. "Really?" He stared at her curiously.

"Um . . . yeah," Jessica said. She bit her lip, not liking the look on Dennis's face. "Um . . . pineapple pizza is one of my favorite things. . . ." Her voice trailed off.

"But you didn't eat any." Dennis's tone was accusing. "Remember? You told me you didn't like pineapple pizza, that only Elizabeth did."

"I . . . I did?" Jessica felt her heart beginning to race. She gave a little laugh. "Has she been pretending she's me again?" Too late she wished she hadn't said that. "I mean—"

Dennis studied her closely as though something about her wasn't quite right. "About our walk," he said slowly. "Where did we go?"

Jessica laughed again, louder this time. "We can talk over old times later," she told Dennis. "Come on—let's go!"

But Dennis's frown deepened. "You're not Jessica," he said accusingly. "You're Elizabeth—aren't you?"

Jessica jumped as if she'd been stung. "What?" she stammered.

"Of course you are." Dennis folded his arms. "I spent enough time with the real Jessica at camp to tell the difference. You're Elizabeth. I know even though you finally got around to taking a shower and washing your hair." He shook his head. "You two aren't quite identical, you know. And I'm positive that you're Elizabeth."

"But I'm *not*," Jessica said helplessly. It was even the truth—for a change. Shouldn't she get *some* credit for telling the truth? "I'm Jessica!" she insisted. "Ask anybody!"

"I might just do that," Dennis said. "But the *real* Jessica told me you liked to pretend to be her.

Especially around April Fools' Day. Which is today."

Jessica felt as if her tongue was made of lead. "But *I'm* not the one who likes to pretend. *She's* the one who—"

"We can settle this easily." Dennis reached into his pocket and pulled out a crumpled red leaf. "Well?" he asked shortly, holding it out for her inspection.

Jessica felt as if she was in a play, only nobody had told her any of her lines. "Well?" she repeated, bewildered. "Well what?"

Dennis gave a barking laugh. "Just as I thought." With a savage gleam in his eye he whirled to face the buses. "You're not Jessica," he scoffed. "Nice try, though, *Elizabeth*. The *real* Jessica is—let me see—ah! There!"

Jessica followed the direction his hand was pointing.

"Standing right over there next to *your* boyfriend. Next to that guy Todd," Dennis continued with satisfaction.

Jessica swallowed hard. She couldn't imagine what was going on. But as she watched Dennis dash for Elizabeth's side, she knew one thing for sure:

Something had gone very, very wrong.

Eighteen

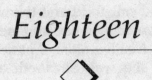

That was absolutely the most humiliating moment of my entire life, Jessica thought two hours later. She lay on the family room couch, feeling sorry for herself.

When Elizabeth hadn't shown Dennis the proper password or whatever it was about that stupid leaf, Dennis had gotten mad and sworn off Wakefields forever. Jessica had railed and yelled at Elizabeth all the way home, and Elizabeth had just sat there in the car with a foolish grin on her face. She'd had the nerve to blame Jessica for the whole thing, even though it was clearly Elizabeth who had messed things up by coming on to Dennis and pretending to be Jessica.

And now Elizabeth had gone off to Casey's with Todd, and Jessica was home alone without a boyfriend. All because of her stupid sister.

"It wasn't like I asked to be used as bait, Jessica," Jessica remembered Elizabeth saying in her prissy voice. *"I mean, you had no right to pretend you were me to begin with!"* She considered various ways of getting back at her sister. Maybe she could pretend to be Elizabeth and call Todd and tell him she'd fallen in love with somebody else and never wanted to see him again. *No. Too unlike Elizabeth.* Maybe she could pretend she was Elizabeth and say dorky things to Todd over the phone. *No. Todd's just dorky enough to like them.* Maybe she could pretend she was Elizabeth and come on to Bruce Patman or somebody and make Todd jealous and—

The doorbell rang.

Jessica considered not answering it. She didn't exactly want to see anybody. But when the bell rang again, she reluctantly got up and walked to the door.

"Hi, Jessica." Aaron stood there, grinning self-consciously, freshly scrubbed and shampooed.

Jessica blinked. Aaron was absolutely the last person she had expected to see. "Um—," she began. Despite herself she couldn't help thinking how handsome he was.

"Can I come in?" Without waiting for an answer Aaron pushed past her and plunked himself down on the family room couch. "Listen, Jessica, there's something I wanted to say."

"There is?" Jessica narrowed her eyes. "I mean . . . what?"

"That I'm sorry," Aaron burst out. "I . . . I wasn't

very nice to you this week and I, um, wanted to, you know, apologize." He didn't quite look Jessica in the eye, but he extended his hand. "So. Friends?"

Jessica hesitated. "You hurt my feelings a lot," she said slowly, remembering how she'd ducked into the brambles to avoid the bear. The bear that wasn't.

"Yeah, well, I got my feelings hurt too," Aaron said cryptically. "In different ways. Like the last night we were there?" He shook his head. "Man, nobody but nobody believed me. And I thought about—you," he said in a rush. "I knew you'd believe me if I told you, but you were—well—" He coughed. "Kind of unavailable."

"Oh," Jessica said. She wondered what Aaron was talking about. "Ah. I see. Because I was sick?"

"Sick?" Aaron shook his head. "Were you sick? You sure didn't *look* sick. I saw you, like, Friday morning, holding hands with that guy—" He coughed again. "Well, never mind."

"Oh." Jessica stared at Aaron. Friday morning. When she was at home with a fever of, like, six million degrees. *She* wasn't holding hands with any guy . . . but someone who looked a whole lot like her must have been.

"I . . . I don't know how you suddenly got to look so good again," Aaron continued. He rubbed his neck and grimaced. "I mean, when I saw you at the beginning of the week, you looked pretty awful."

Jessica drew her mouth into a tight line. Maybe she wouldn't accept his apology after all.

"But later . . ." Aaron shrugged. "I guess I realized what I was missing."

Then again, maybe she would. "Aaron . . . ," Jessica began.

Aaron paid no attention. "And when that guy said he had the hots for you—"

"He did?" Jessica couldn't help interjecting.

Aaron looked up, surprised. "Well, Jessica, I *saw* you," he said. "You two were walking around hand in hand. . . ." His voice trailed off.

"I see." Jessica's mind whirled. Maybe—just maybe—what Elizabeth had done wasn't so awful. Maybe, in a weird way, she'd done Jessica a favor. . . .

"So I just wanted to know," Aaron went on, "if it was, like, all over between us. If you and Dennis are sort of together. Because if you are—" His eyes traveled to meet Jessica's. "Then I'll just leave you alone. It's not like I treated you great or anything, I know. But if you think you might want to be my sort-of girlfriend again, then . . ." He swallowed hard. "Then I have a different idea," he said in a strangled voice.

Jessica could have laughed out loud. So Elizabeth hanging all over Dennis had done some good after all! She stared at Aaron. Suddenly she remembered all his good qualities. All the things that had attracted her to him to begin with. His sense of humor, and the way that he'd sometimes do nice things for her, and his good looks, especially now that he'd taken a shower, and the fun times they'd had. . . .

"Sure," she said, trying not to sound too eager. "Dennis is a nice guy, but I don't think it's going to work out."

Aaron breathed a sigh of relief.

"So what exactly did you have in mind?" Jessica asked.

"Just—this." Aaron stood and walked quickly to Jessica's side. Jessica watched his face come closer and closer to her own until his lips met hers.

And then she realized that he was kissing her.

With her free hand she encircled his neck and pulled him closer. *My first kiss!* she thought.

She shut her eyes, enjoying the moment.

It wasn't how she'd planned that first kiss, with the moonlight dancing in the background and the rows of tall whispering pine trees and the sky full of stars. But Jessica smiled as Aaron gently released her.

After that camp experience there was no way she would have wanted that first kiss to be outdoors anyway!

Bantam Books in the SWEET VALLEY TWINS series.
Ask your bookseller for the books you have missed.

#1	BEST FRIENDS	#24	JUMPING TO CONCLUSIONS
#2	TEACHER'S PET	#25	STANDING OUT
#3	THE HAUNTED HOUSE	#26	TAKING CHARGE
#4	CHOOSING SIDES	#27	TEAMWORK
#5	SNEAKING OUT	#28	APRIL FOOL!
#6	THE NEW GIRL	#29	JESSICA AND THE BRAT ATTACK
#7	THREE'S A CROWD	#30	PRINCESS ELIZABETH
#8	FIRST PLACE	#31	JESSICA'S BAD IDEA
#9	AGAINST THE RULES	#32	JESSICA ONSTAGE
#10	ONE OF THE GANG	#33	ELIZABETH'S NEW HERO
#11	BURIED TREASURE	#34	JESSICA, THE ROCK STAR
#12	KEEPING SECRETS	#35	AMY'S PEN PAL
#13	STRETCHING THE TRUTH	#36	MARY IS MISSING
#14	TUG OF WAR	#37	THE WAR BETWEEN THE TWINS
#15	THE OLDER BOY	#38	LOIS STRIKES BACK
#16	SECOND BEST	#39	JESSICA AND THE MONEY MIX-UP
#17	BOYS AGAINST GIRLS	#40	DANNY MEANS TROUBLE
#18	CENTER OF ATTENTION	#41	THE TWINS GET CAUGHT
#19	THE BULLY	#42	JESSICA'S SECRET
#20	PLAYING HOOKY	#43	ELIZABETH'S FIRST KISS
#21	LEFT BEHIND	#44	AMY MOVES IN
#22	OUT OF PLACE	#45	LUCY TAKES THE REINS
#23	CLAIM TO FAME	#46	MADEMOISELLE JESSICA

Sweet Valley Twins Super Editions

#1	THE CLASS TRIP	#5	LILA'S SECRET VALENTINE
#2	HOLIDAY MISCHIEF	#6	THE TWINS TAKE PARIS
#3	THE BIG CAMP SECRET	#7	JESSICA'S ANIMAL INSTINCTS
#4	THE UNICORNS GO HAWAIIAN	#8	JESSICA'S FIRST KISS

Sweet Valley Twins Super Chiller Editions

#1	THE CHRISTMAS GHOST	#6	THE CURSE OF THE GOLDEN HEART
#2	THE GHOST IN THE GRAVEYARD	#7	THE HAUNTED BURIAL GROUND
#3	THE CARNIVAL GHOST	#8	THE SECRET OF THE MAGIC PEN
#4	THE GHOST IN THE BELL TOWER	#9	EVIL ELIZABETH
#5	THE CURSE OF THE RUBY NECKLACE		

Sweet Valley Twins Magna Editions

THE MAGIC CHRISTMAS	A CHRISTMAS WITHOUT ELIZABETH
BIG FOR CHRISTMAS	#100 IF I DIE BEFORE I WAKE

#47	JESSICA'S NEW LOOK	#77	TODD RUNS AWAY
#48	MANDY MILLER FIGHTS BACK	#78	STEVEN THE ZOMBIE
#49	THE TWINS' LITTLE SISTER	#79	JESSICA'S BLIND DATE
#50	JESSICA AND THE SECRET STAR	#80	THE GOSSIP WAR
#51	ELIZABETH THE IMPOSSIBLE	#81	ROBBERY AT THE MALL
#52	BOOSTER BOYCOTT	#82	STEVEN'S ENEMY
#53	THE SLIME THAT ATE SWEET VALLEY	#83	AMY'S SECRET SISTER
		#84	ROMEO AND 2 JULIETS
#54	THE BIG PARTY WEEKEND	#85	ELIZABETH THE SEVENTH-GRADER
#55	BROOKE AND HER ROCK-STAR MOM	#86	IT CAN'T HAPPEN HERE
		#87	THE MOTHER-DAUGHTER SWITCH
#56	THE WAKEFIELDS STRIKE IT RICH	#88	STEVEN GETS EVEN
#57	BIG BROTHER'S IN LOVE!	#89	JESSICA'S COOKIE DISASTER
#58	ELIZABETH AND THE ORPHANS	#90	THE COUSIN WAR
#59	BARNYARD BATTLE	#91	DEADLY VOYAGE
#60	CIAO, SWEET VALLEY!	#92	ESCAPE FROM TERROR ISLAND
#61	JESSICA THE NERD	#93	THE INCREDIBLE MADAME JESSICA
#62	SARAH'S DAD AND SOPHIA'S MOM	#94	DON'T TALK TO BRIAN
#63	POOR LILA!	#95	THE BATTLE OF THE CHEERLEADERS
#64	THE CHARM SCHOOL MYSTERY		
#65	PATTY'S LAST DANCE	#96	ELIZABETH THE SPY
#66	THE GREAT BOYFRIEND SWITCH	#97	TOO SCARED TO SLEEP
#67	JESSICA THE THIEF	#98	THE BEAST IS WATCHING YOU
#68	THE MIDDLE SCHOOL GETS MARRIED	#99	THE BEAST MUST DIE
		#100	IF I DIE BEFORE I WAKE (MAGNA)
#69	WON'T SOMEONE HELP ANNA?	#101	TWINS IN LOVE
#70	PSYCHIC SISTERS	#102	THE MYSTERIOUS DR. Q
#71	JESSICA SAVES THE TREES	#103	ELIZABETH SOLVES IT ALL
#72	THE LOVE POTION	#104	BIG BROTHER'S IN LOVE AGAIN
#73	LILA'S MUSIC VIDEO	#105	JESSICA'S LUCKY MILLIONS
#74	ELIZABETH THE HERO		
#75	JESSICA AND THE EARTHQUAKE		
#76	YOURS FOR A DAY		

SIGN UP FOR THE SWEET VALLEY HIGH® FAN CLUB!

Hey, girls! Get all the gossip on Sweet Valley High's® most popular teenagers when you join our fantastic Fan Club! As a member, you'll get all of this really cool stuff:

- Membership Card with your own personal Fan Club ID number
- A Sweet Valley High® Secret Treasure Box
- Sweet Valley High® Stationery
- Official Fan Club Pencil (for secret note writing!)
- Three Bookmarks
- A "Members Only" Door Hanger
- Two Skeins of J. & P. Coats® Embroidery Floss with flower barrette instruction leaflet

- Two editions of *The Oracle* newsletter
- Plus exclusive Sweet Valley High® product offers, special savings, contests, and much more!

Be the first to find out what Jessica & Elizabeth Wakefield are up to by joining the Sweet Valley High® Fan Club for the one-year membership fee of only $6.25 each for U.S. residents, $8.25 for Canadian residents (U.S. currency). Includes shipping & handling.

Send a check or money order (do not send cash) made payable to "Sweet Valley High® Fan Club" along with this form to:

SWEET VALLEY HIGH® FAN CLUB, BOX 3919-B, SCHAUMBURG, IL 60168-3919

NAME_____
(Please print clearly)

ADDRESS_____

CITY_____ STATE _____ ZIP_____
(Required)

AGE _____ BIRTHDAY_____ /_____ /_____

Offer good while supplies last. Allow 6-8 weeks after check clearance for delivery. Addresses without ZIP codes cannot be honored. Offer good in USA & Canada only. Void where prohibited by law.
©1993 by Francine Pascal   LCI-1383-193